A PIRATE'S RANSOM

GERRI BROUSSEAU

Vicki

Enjoy the Journey

Gerri B

SOUL MATE PUBLISHING

New York

A PIRATE'S RANSOM
Copyright©2012
GERRI BROUSSEAU

Cover Design by Rae Monet, Inc.

This book is a work of fiction. The names, characters, places, and incidents are the products of the author's imagination or are used fictitiously. Any resemblance to actual events, business establishments, locales, or persons, living or dead, is entirely coincidental.

Published in the United States of America by
Soul Mate Publishing
P.O. Box 24
Macedon, New York, 14502

ISBN: 978-1-61935-218-6
eBook ISBN: 978-1-61935-118-9

www.SoulMatePublishing.com
The publisher does not have any control over and does not assume any responsibility for author or third-party Web sites or their content.

This book is dedicated to Mark and Sarah.

Thanks for believing in me and helping me

believe in myself.

Acknowledgements

I would like to thank my mentor and friend, author Susan Hanniford Crowley for all her help with putting the wind in *Pirate's* sails. I could not have done this without her. Thanks for picking me up when I felt deflated, for helping me believe in myself, and especially for pushing me to contact publishers. I also want to thank Peter Andrews. Without your workshop on fast fiction, I would never have written *Pirate's*. I especially want to thank Debby Gilbert for saying "yes" and for helping me polish *Pirate's* to perfection!

Chapter 1

"Father, how could you?" I shrieked, slamming my fist down on the wooden kitchen table in our island home.

"Think of it, my dear. You'll be a Duchess," he said, leaning back in his chair and giving me that crooked smile of his.

"Yes, and I will also be married to a man I have never met. If mother were alive, this would not be happening. She would never have allowed this." I paced back and forth in our cramped kitchen, anger boiling in my gut.

"Mind your tongue, girl. Your mother, God rest her sainted soul, would see it for what it is, our salvation. Now stop thinking only of yourself. Think of all the riches. We shall want for nothing."

"I want for nothing now, Father. I was not brought up in the Courts of London, but here, on this Island, thanks to your indiscretions with the Viceroy's wife." I felt the worm of guilt curl in my stomach. I knew it was disrespectful, but my anger gave rise to the outburst. Shock, and something else, maybe a flash of guilt, passed over his handsome aging face.

"You thought I didn't know? Just because I was only ten when we were forced to leave London? Believe me, I was quite aware of why we were leaving." He cast his eyes downward. I knew I had crossed the line, but pressed him further. "What were you thinking in agreeing to this match, Father? I have not had the opportunity to master the ways of a fine Lady. You know we live modestly here. We dress plainly. I do not have fancy gowns. I wear simple cotton skirts and blouses, similar to what I have on now. How do you intend to pass me off as a wealthy Countess?"

"Never forget, Catherine, although we no longer possess wealth, you are a Countess. As for your meeting with the duke, we shall use what little coin we have left to purchase a few fancy gowns to make you look the part of the rich Countess that ol' Duke thinks you to be," he said with a wink. The same wink he always used when he was up to no good. A shudder ran through me. *Here we go again*, I thought, *only this time, the wager at stake is my future!*

Then his words echoed in my mind. "Old?" I bellowed, my heart plummeting. "Exactly how old is the Duke?" My stomach turned at the thought of what my father had gotten me into.

"Just a figure of speech, that. Besides, what does it matter? His wealth will last long beyond his years. I have made a fine match for you. Wentworth Simmons is the Duke of Devonshire and it be told his coffers run deep."

"Yes, and I am certain you are anxious to be swimming in that deep pool."

"Why, you ungrateful girl. You should be happy."

Happy, I thought. *He's signed my death warrant and may as well have sentenced me to prison.* Sighing deeply, I drew the drapes closed for the last time on the view of the bay from my bedroom window. We'd had that fateful conversation two months ago, and ever since that time I'd had no success getting Father to change his mind.

"You 'bout ready to go, Miss?" My maid's sweet voice broke into my thoughts, her Cockney accent a comforting and familiar song.

"I suppose," I whispered.

"Don't be sad, Miss. We'll be back in London in a fortnight, and you'll be presented to grand society and attendin' fancy balls and gay parties, ye will."

"Yes, and preparing to be married to an old man. Oh, Mary, my life is over," I said with a sob.

"Oh, now, Miss, don't be thinkin' on it like that." The timid maid rushed to my side and rested her hand upon my arm.

"I suppose I should be lucky to have any husband with these rough and calloused hands and my thin form."

"Ye worked hard keepin' them horses, Miss."

"And I have a fine tan and the muscles of a man to show for it. I'll never fit in with the pale skinned, genteel ladies of the Court in London. I shall be a laughing stock."

"Don't ye be talkin' like that, Miss."

"We could have afforded to have a proper stable boy if Father could have only stopped his drinking and gaming."

"Ye loved them horses, and ye took right good care of 'em, ye did."

"Thank you, Mary. But it didn't matter, for in the end Father sold them." The sting of tears threatened my eyes.

"Aye, Miss, for the coin to buy ye new gowns. I know yer sad, but better to not be thinkin' on it over much. Things will all work out . . . they always do . . . you'll see."

"Oh Mary, I'm so thankful you are coming to London with me." I managed a smile.

"I been with ye since ye was a babe. Not likely I would be left behind. Yer father is a kind man. Really, Miss. He's only thinkin' on makin' a fine future for ye."

She's right, of course, I thought as I pulled myself together. But she failed to mention the fine future he also planned to enjoy. Dabbing my eyes with a lace handkerchief, I drew myself up tall and reminded myself that I must act according to my station.

Standing outside in the courtyard before our island home, I was grateful to have my maid beside me. Dressed in her gray travel uniform, she took charge of my belongings. I looked around, taking in every detail. Wanting to remember everything, from the lush island flowers with a fragrance like perfume to the slant of the roof and the wide veranda. To the palm trees that surrounded the house and colorful birds that nested in their branches. I wanted to commit everything to memory. The sun shown warm upon my skin, yet a chill ran through me. I felt numb and remained silent watching the servants load the wagon with the trunks holding my belongings. *Some grand Countess I am*, I thought. My entire life had been summed up in those few trunks. As much as I hated having been forced to leave London in disgrace eight years ago to come here to this strange and beautiful island, I dreaded returning there now even more. Sadness overwhelmed me as I realized I would never return to my home.

"Come now, Catherine," my father said, taking my arm. "Let us be on our way. They will not hold the ship for us. If we do not take our leave immediately, I fear *The Tempest* will be underway without us."

Tears stung my eyes when I looked at him, but I refused to allow myself to cry. I knew despite my dread and all my misgivings, I could not ask him to change his mind. As unfair as it was, I knew this was our last hope to resolve our tenuous financial situation. *I cannot disappoint my father. He is counting on me.*

The activity of boarding *The Tempest* and getting under way seemed a blur in my memory. Mary kept an appropriate distance as I stood at the rail of the ship gazing out at the expanse of ocean spreading out before me. Watching the seabirds fly freely above, I longed to be among them, but I was trapped, and I was angry. With land now fading into the distance, the briny smell of the sea flowed around me and a strong breeze forced my long, dark hair back and away from my face. The cool sea spray kissed my cheeks, but did little to cool my temper. *How much trouble had I been to Father since Mother's death that he thought to pawn me off to the first man to petition for my hand?* The burn of anger rushed through me, and I stomped my foot knowing I was powerless to stop my upcoming nuptials, and dreading the wedding night in particular, wed to a stranger Father had referred to as "old," yet I would never disobey or disgrace him.

Pulling my deep blue cloak more snuggly around me, I whispered into the wind, "I wish something would happen to prevent me from reaching England and from having to marry the old duke." Closing my eyes, I imagined my words traveling up into the sky, a prayer being carried away on the trade winds.

The ship headed north toward England, and now with no land in sight, the waves grew to enormous heights, causing the ship to pitch and roll, as did my stomach.

Maybe I had better head back below deck now, I thought, as my stomach threatened to give my lunch up to the fish. Just when I was about to face away from the rail, a flash of white on the horizon caught my eye. "Another ship?" I whispered, and, holding tightly to the rail, I froze in place and watched the magnificent sight, its sails stark white against the deep blue of the sea and sky. I could not tear my eyes away from the magnificence of the splendid vessel, also being tossed about on the ocean. *Where were they heading? Surely their destination would be preferable to mine.* As I watched the bow glide gracefully across the water I wished I were on that ship going anywhere else.

"I have never seen anything more beautiful than a ship in full sail upon the open ocean," I said.

"Aye, that it be, but ye an' yer maid best be 'eadin' below deck now, Countess," a strongly accented male voice warned.

"Why?" I asked, startled, and turned to find one of the crewmen standing behind me. His shaggy gray hair hung from beneath his faded red cap and the lower half of his face sported a bristle of a white beard.

"Until we can figure wot flag that there ship be flyin', ye best remain unseen, Countess. I don't be meanin' to alarm ye, me Lady, but there be talk that pirates roam in these waters." His strong Cockney accent sounded so similar to Mary's.

"Pirates?" I faced back to watch the approaching vessel. *And I had expected this would be a boring journey.*

"Aye, me Lady."

"Pirates!" Mary cried, rushing to my side. "Oh Miss, we best take heed to the gentleman's word 'n get ourselves below."

"Nonsense, Mary. Look at the great distance between us. It would surely take a day's time at least before that ship could travel the distance to where we are now, and by then, we shall be long away from here."

"Oh, I don't know Miss. Wot if it truly be Pirates? Mister Smith be likely the one who knows more about these matters and he be tellin' us to go below. We best heed his words."

"You go on ahead, Mary. I wish to remain here for just a moment longer. I shall join you below directly."

"If the Captain o' that vessel had a mind to, that ship could be upon us in no time. I do believe ye should be listenin' to yer maid," Smith put in.

"Thank you, Mister Smith."

"Ye be certain it be all right to leave ye unattended, Miss?" Mary asked timidly.

"Certainly, Mary. You go ahead. Go to your cabin. I shall be in mine before you have even had the time to remove your cloak. I swear it."

"As ye wish, Miss. Thank ye, me Lady." Bobbing her head and drawing her cloak tighter around her, Mary scurried across the deck and down the stairs that led to her cabin.

Turning back to the rail, all thoughts of my beloved maid slipped from my mind. I couldn't tear my eyes away from the sight of the majestic ship, which had now turned and appeared to be heading in our direction.

The beautiful white sails strained in the wind as the great ship drew closer. The bow neared, and I could tell it was a much larger vessel than *The Tempest*, cutting through the water with such swiftness and grace, I found myself mesmerized.

"Miss," Smith said frantically, taking hold of my arm. "I fear for ye. It ain't safe. Get yerself below and stay locked in yer cabin, an' no matter wot, don't be openin' that door."

Grabbing my arm more securely, he dragged me along behind him like I was a rag doll. The entire crew suddenly seemed on high alert, with everyone rushing to their stations and the captain shouting orders.

"Turn it to the wind," the Captain yelled and in moments, the ship changed course. And as the wind took greater hold of the sails, the ship tilted slightly and picked up speed.

"Father? Where is my father?" I shouted to Mr. Smith over the raging wind and the loud flapping of the sails as he dragged me toward the hatch leading below deck and down to my cabin.

"He be already locked away in 'is cabin, if he got any sense to hisself."

I followed Smith along the narrow passageway as frantic shouts from above deck filled the air. But my heart raced when I heard the dreaded word shouted from above. "Pirates!"

Smith opened the door, shoved me into my cabin, and handing me the key, he said, "Lock it now, Miss, and don't be openin' it even if the devil hisself be a knockin', cuz if we don't outrun them pirates, and they takes the ship, that be who'll be at your door."

"Will you fight them, then?"

"Nay, Miss. Their number likely be too great. Our only hope is to out run 'em. But, our small size will be to our advantage," he said with a wink. So like my father. Giving me that wink to assure me of yet another scheme that would never work. A shudder ran down my spine at the thought of it.

"Mister Smith, what will happen if we are not able to outrun them?"

"Do ye know how to use a pistol, Miss?"

"What?" Nerves danced in my stomach.

"A pistol, me Lady." He shoved the cold firearm into my hand. "If them pirates take this ship, take aim, n' shoot whoever comes thru the door. Now lock it!"

He hurried out of my cabin, pulled the door closed behind him, and was gone. With trembling fingers, I shoved the key into the lock and turned it. Backing away, my mouth went dry and my eyes frantically scanned the small cabin for another way out, but there was none.

The weight of the pistol was uncomfortable in my hand, and I had no idea how to use it, yet I could not bring myself to lay it aside.

Rushing to the small round window, I peered out, straining to get a glimpse of what was going on.

The crew scurrying around sounded like thunder above me, and I thought the ceiling might cave in. Fear-filled voices shouting from the deck echoed off the walls of the compact cabin, and my heart thundered. I struggled to breathe, yet I was unable to drag myself away from the window.

The ship pitched and turned, forcing me to take a few quick steps to keep from falling. My heartbeat shot up as waves crested the window, and we seemed to pick up even more speed. Books and other items crashed from their shelves down to the cabin floor with the deepened tilt of the ship. Stumbling, I held tight to both the window casing and the pistol, pressing my face against the glass, frantically scanning the sea for the sight of white sails.

A shadow passed across my face and I drew back with a start. The huge pirate ship drew alongside us. On legs that felt like jelly, I slowly backed away from the window and into the shadows of what I felt would surely become my prison. Our diminutive ship, having been easily overtaken, slowed and eventually stood stone still, bobbing like a cork on the tide.

With rapid breath, I stood in the center of the cabin, searching for a place to hide. The blast of cannon fire made me jump, but the wood-shattering sound that vibrated to the core of the ship made the knot in my stomach rise to my throat. The numbing silence that followed hummed in my ears. There was no more cannon fire and no subsequent gunshots, only the sound of my heart hammering as I listened for some clue of what was going on above, but the only sound was that of the waves lapping against the side of the ship and the muted voices in conversation rumbling above me. The hair rose on the back of my neck at the frightening realization that we had indeed been captured by pirates. And for the first time since my mother's death, I fell to my knees and with tears streaming down my cheeks, I prayed.

Chapter 2

The sound of the splintering wood of doors being blown open was accompanied by heavy footfalls along the passageway toward my cabin.

"Take yer filthy hands off me, ye vermin." Mary's scream was followed by the raunchy laughter of several men.

My heart hammered and my legs trembled in my effort to rise to my feet, yet I was determined to face the approaching threat with the dignity of my station. Holding my breath, my eyes fixed to the door latch, I waited.

"It be locked, same as the others," a rough male voice shouted.

"Blast it off its hinges. You heard the Captain's orders." The deafening sound of a pistol shot and splintering wood as a ball struck the lock nearly sent me to my knees.

The smell of gunpowder burned my nostrils and brought tears to my eyes. I struggled to contain my increasing fears but remained frozen in the center of my cabin, shaking and suddenly feeling in desperate need of a chamber pot as the door, now with the lock blown apart, slowly swung inward.

"Well, well, wot 'ave we 'ere?" the rugged and scruffy man asked as he scanned me up and down. His hungry stare made me feel as if I stood naked before him, and heat burned my cheeks.

Stepping into my cabin, he was followed closely by another pirate, who dragged Mary along with him, despite the fact that she was kicking and punching.

"You best not be layin' a 'and on her!" Mary screamed.

"It's quite all right, Mary." Despite my knocking knees, I managed to hold myself tall and prayed they did not hear my heart thundering.

"And who might ye be?" the scruffy one asked.

"That there be Lady Catherine Nettleton, Countess of Dorset, she be, on her way to London to be wed to his Grace, the Duke of Devonshire," Mary said, a hint of pride in her voice.

My heart sank. Her outburst had ruined any hope we may have had of duping the pirates.

"Well, well, yer Ladyship. Our Captain requests the honor of yer presence aboard our fine vessel," Scruffy said, taking a step closer.

I suddenly recalled the pistol in my hand, and with shaking limbs, I raised it and pointed it directly at his chest. Upon seeing the firearm, he raised his hands, not above his head, but before him as if to catch a ball tossed to him by a child.

"Shoot him, Miss," Mary squawked, thrashing wildly despite her captor's attempts to keep her still.

"Now yer Ladyship, there be no need to be shootin' no one." Scruffy gave a gap-toothed grin.

A shiver of revulsion ran down my spine and my already queasy stomach curdled when I got a whiff of him.

"If you take one step further, I swear I shall shoot you."

"Aye, I be certain that be yer intent," he responded. Yet, my lack of knowledge of the use of a firearm must have been blatantly apparent to him as he continued, "But that pistol ye be wavin' be useless without a flint." Reaching up, he took the pistol from my shaking hands with ease.

"There now, yer Ladyship, as I be sayin' . . . the Captain he be a'waitin'." Grabbing my upper arm, he yanked me toward the door. "An' the Captain, he 'ates to be kept waitin'," he said and pulled me along the passageway, then dragged me up to the main deck.

The bright sun blinded me and, raising my hand to shade my eyes, I saw the entire crew had been assembled, my father among them, lined up and being held at gunpoint by a band of shaggy and ragged men. The beautiful sails of our tiny ship had been shredded and the main mast lay broken and hanging over the side, its tip plunging into the water. Scruffy shoved me into the line with the crew, and I felt a small measure of comfort to find Mary standing beside me.

"Miss," she whimpered, "I fear for our lives."

I took her trembling hand in mine. "Don't worry, Mary. There is nothing aboard this ship of any value to these men. I feel certain they will leave us in peace." *Am I trying to convince her, or myself?*

"Nay, yer Ladyship, that's where ye be mistaken,'" Scruffy said as a sinister smile spread slowly across his thin lips.

I gasped for breath. My lungs burned as if I were drowning. His gaze raked over me from head to toe, making me feel violated and dirty without even a touch. When I could no longer bear it, I averted my face away from his. He stood so close to me now, I felt his warm breath on my neck.

"Ye smell like a rose in full bloom, ye do," he muttered in my ear.

The rank smell of him caused my stomach to roll, but I dared not rebuke him for fear of some worse treatment. Trying to hold my breath, I took a step back away from him, and my back slammed up against the thick expanse of the bottom of the broken and splintered mast.

Moving even closer, he pinned me between him and the mast, then placed his hands upon my shoulders.

"I wonder wot yer kiss be like," he said in a tone little more than a whisper, and I was unable to control the shudder that ran through me. Placing his grimy fingers under my chin, he turned my face toward his. It was all I could do not to vomit at the odor of him and the fetid stench of his rotting teeth. Swallowing hard, I forced down the bile rising in my throat.

"Please." A hoarse whisper managed to escape me.

"Aye, yer Ladyship. I aim to please ye," he whispered.

"Take yer filthy 'ands off her!" Mary shrieked. She tried to rush to my aid, but two of the pirates grabbed her and held her back.

Scruffy's face was so close to mine that nary an inch remained between us. His black eyes burned into my flesh, like a starving man eyeing his next meal. Leaning in closer still, he pressed his filthy body against mine and placing one dirty hand upon my waist, he whispered, "Do ye have any idea how long it's been since I had a woman?"

The band of miscreants cheered him on, and I realized for the first time that my virtue might indeed be lost. Tears pooled in my eyes and I averted my face away from his, unable to tolerate his closeness a moment longer. His grimy hand moved from my waist and inched up toward the bodice of my gown as he began slobbering kisses upon my neck. The shiver that ran through me was visible to anyone watching.

"And a beauty such as yerself . . . aye . . . a pleasure it'll be."

Just as his hand reached my breast, the sharp sound of an object hurling swiftly toward us rang out. The air stirred beside my head, followed by the vibration of something slamming into the mast very close to my ear. Scruffy jumped back at the sound of the sword still vibrating in the wood only inches from his head.

"Mister Taylor." A deep and dangerous voice echoed over the vibrating sword and the heads of the men who now fell silent before him. "I believe I gave explicit instructions that the prisoner not be touched."

"Beggin' yer pardon, Captain . . . I was just havin' a little feel o' the girl. No harm done, no harm done," he stammered as he backed away.

I looked up toward the sound of the dark and dangerous voice, but the owner stood above me, up upon the rail, and with the sun at his back offered only the darkness of his shadow.

"If any man among you cares to disobey my orders, you may feel free to remain here, upon the disabled *Tempest*. Otherwise, gather the prisoner and make way back to *The Lady Victoria*. Mister Taylor, bring the Countess to my cabin . . . unharmed," he commanded, and then he turned away.

The scruffy Mister Taylor grabbed hold of my arm, but I tore it from his grasp.

"I'm not going anywhere with you," I hissed at him through clenched teeth. He leaned closer, bringing his thin and grimy face within inches of mine.

"Aye, ye be, Countess . . . like it or no," he replied. Grabbing my arm, a little more roughly this time, he dragged me across the deck.

"Captain," I shouted as loudly as I could.

Every man upon the deck froze, then looked in their Captain's direction. The Captain turned back to face me, and with the sun in my eyes, I still could not make out his features.

"A request, Milady?" he asked with a hint of amusement in his voice.

"Yes, if you please, Sir, kindly permit me to have my maid, Mary, accompany me, for propriety's sake," I said in a strong clear voice, resounding with a courage I certainly didn't feel.

He laughed and said, "Are there any others among you who wish to accompany the Countess?"

Silence filled the air, and I chanced a glance at my

father, who cast his eyes downward and said not a word. *Coward.*

"I am certain there is at least one among you who would be competent enough to deliver a message to the Duke of Devonshire. Kindly advise His Grace that if he wishes to ever see his lovely bride again, he shall pay a pirate's ransom," the pirate lord's powerful voice commanded.

"Beggin' yer pardon, Sir," Smith muttered, taking a tentative step toward the pirate lord, "but do ye mind tellin' us wot amount a coin a pirate's ransom be?"

"Ah, Smith, there you are. You have been most helpful in assisting me here today, and your reward awaits you aboard *The Lady*. As for His Grace, Wentworth Simmons is quite aware of what my ransom demands are. Now, Countess, would you care to extend an invitation to any others to accompany you before we depart?"

My mouth dropped open as I watched the wiry Mister Smith, my betrayer, scamper across the plank and onto the huge pirate ship. Snapping my jaw closed, I allowed my eyes to sweep the remainder of the crew and I dared a glance once again at my father, whose gaze met mine briefly. But in that scant moment, I recognized his silent plea, begging me not to name him.

Realizing the pirate lord awaited my reply, I uttered softly, "No, Sir. Just my maid, if you would be so kind."

"Very well, Milady, as you wish." Without another word, he strode off, his large frame disappearing into the setting sun.

Rough hands grabbed me and passed me from hand to hand, lifting me high into the air above their heads, like a sack of grain being carried across the plank that rested between our tiny ship and the grand pirate vessel.

My teeth jarred as I was set down roughly upon the deck, and finding my balance, I turned just in time to see the plank being pulled away from *The Tempest*. My chest heaved and my breath came rapidly from scrambling and trying to pull away from the grasp of the vile Mister Taylor. His fingers tightened like irons around my arm, and the helplessness of my situation tightened its grip around my heart. I gazed upon the stark and drawn face of my father standing among the crew, helpless on the deck of the disabled vessel, and fear nearly closed my throat, choking off my breath.

"Wot o' them others, Captain?" Mister Taylor asked, following my gaze.

"Leave them," the eloquent Captain called back over his shoulder as he strode away from us.

My limbs shook, and I couldn't bring myself to face my captors. My heart hammered and I tried to rein in my fear. Mustering a measure of courage, I chanced a sideways glance through lowered lashes at the pirate lord.

My hooded eyes followed him and although his back was to me, I was surprised to find he was not at all what I expected. I thought certainly he would be dirty and covered in filthy rags, much as his crew, but he wasn't. He stood at least a head above any of his men and wore a clean, stark white shirt, which clung to his broad shoulders. His raven hair gleamed in the sunlight, despite the fact that it was tied back in a black ribbon, and his long legs were covered in dark trousers that seemed to stretch downward and melt into the tops of shiny black boots. No, he was not what I expected at all.

But when he neared the passage descending into the bowels of the ship, he turned to face his crew and despite my shaking knees, my breath caught in my throat and it was all I could do to stifle a gasp. Handsome was not the word to describe the man who faced me, for it would fall short in telling of the look of him. His deeply tanned face was smooth and clean-shaven, perfect but for the thin scar gracing his left cheekbone and spoke of an underlying danger that only added to his appeal. What really struck me though and held my stare were his eyes . . . deep green, sparkling as the sea and framed with the haze of thick dark lashes. His lazy gaze wandered over me, and a tiny hint of a grin captured just the corner of his lips when his eyes finally met mine. Drawing his attention away from me, he called out orders to his crew.

"All hands to your stations—hoist the sails. Mister Beckett, take the wheel," he yelled and turned again to descend the stairway, when almost as an afterthought he called over his shoulder, "Mister Taylor, bring the prisoner to my quarters."

Chapter 3

My knees knocked beneath my skirts, but I held my head high and with all the decorum of a Countess, I swept into the Pirate Lord's quarters. I heard tales of what pirates did to women, but I was driven by a determination not to allow him to see my fear.

"Welcome aboard my humble ship, Countess. There is no need to be afraid. It is not my intention to harm you. Please, take a seat," he said, indicating a plush armchair. Then facing my jailer, he added, "That will be all, Mister Taylor."

"Aye, Captain." My tormenter started to back out of the opened door.

"Mister Taylor," the Captain said.

"Aye."

"Would you kindly see to it that some tea is brought in?"

"Aye, Captain, that I will," he murmured, then continued backing out of the room and closed the door behind him. My heart lurched when the latch clicked into place, but I tried to remain calm.

"I assume you like tea, Countess?"

"Yes, tea would be lovely," I answered in a shaking voice. I couldn't help but wonder why he was extending all these pleasantries, when he'd kidnapped me and was now holding me prisoner. The situation seemed nearly humorous, and with my added nervousness, a giggle bubbled out of me.

"You find humor in something, Countess?" He cocked his head to the side.

"I merely wonder why you seem to be extending pleasantries when, in fact, I am your prisoner."

"Please, do not think of yourself as my prisoner, Milady. You are free to venture about the ship, however, although I have given the strictest of orders that you are not to be touched, I must caution you not to venture too far from my side. Anyone who violates my orders must answer to me, yet I fear the sight of you would test the will of any man, let alone my crew. I'm afraid it has been quite some time since we have made port."

A sheepish grin captured his lips and his clear green eyes danced with amusement. My cheeks burned in a flush of heat that stung from my neck to my hairline as the meaning of his statement dawned on me, and I looked down to my lap. Trying to avoid eye contact with the handsome pirate, I allowed my gaze to travel around his vast quarters.

The dark wood of the walls gave a rich feeling to the room, and I couldn't help but note the elegant furnishings and masculine décor of the cabin. One corner of the room was occupied by a grand desk, the size of which I had never seen. There was a long dining table made of dark wood surrounded by plush chairs in the opposite corner. But my pulse raced when I noticed the oversized bed consuming a good portion of the room. When I glanced at my captor, his amusement was written all over his face, and his eyes sparkled with it.

I was thankful for the knock upon the door with the delivery of our tea, but butterflies stirred in my stomach as soon as we were alone again. My captor half sat, half leaned lazily against the edge of the table and let his eyes travel over me.

"Where are you taking me?" I demanded.

"That depends, Milady," he answered distractedly, giving some attention to the tea tray.

"On what?"

"On whether my ransom demands are met."

"And if they are not?"

"I have to admit, I have not considered that possibility."

"Perhaps you should have given that part of your plan a bit more consideration, Captain."

"Milady, you must think me callous, but I have failed to introduce myself. Please forgive me. I am Edmund Drake, Captain of this fine vessel." He rose and took my hand.

Rising to my feet on legs of jelly, my eyes met his as he brought my hand to his lips. His kiss was soft upon my fingers and my breath caught in my throat. His crystal green eyes sparkled with a smile he seemed to be suppressing. *Get a hold of yourself. This cad is so cock sure of himself, I imagine he has had this effect on many a maiden.* I snatched my hand away from his as if I had been burned.

"How dare you!" I gasped.

Ignoring my outrage, he continued. "Milady, I would never be so bold as to accuse you of being ill-mannered, but you have yet to tell me your name."

"My name is Catherine Nettleton, as if you did not already know. But you may refer to me as Countess or Lady Catherine," I snapped.

He chuckled. "Very well, Lady Catherine. Would you care for some tea?"

He's quite enjoying this game of cat and mouse.

"No, thank you. What I would care for is to be shown to my cabin."

His gaze casually roamed over me, settling upon the bodice of my gown.

I crossed my arms over my chest and glared at him.

"Why, my dear Countess, you're standing in it."

"How kind of you to forfeit your quarters for me, Captain," I said, a trickle of unease skittering along my spine.

"Forfeit, Nay, Countess." His gaze held a hint of something I did not care for. "Share. I shall share my quarters with you."

"Share!" I exclaimed, horrified, and my eyes flew to the one oversized bed.

"As I have said, for your own safety, you should never venture far from my side. Tea, Milady?"

Chapter 4

I remained fixed in place, not quite knowing what to do, but wishing I could slap that cocky smirk from his handsome face. I gave him my most authoritative glare, which usually sent household staff into silence, but only produced the rumble of a deep chuckle from the pirate. He did not spare me another glance while he poured the tea and placed a scone upon a delicate china plate.

How odd, I thought as I watched him. He seems so out of place. An eloquent gentleman pouring tea into fine china, not in the elegant drawing room of a fine home or grand salon in London, but here on this ship accompanied by a band of dirty pirates.

"Won't you join me, Milady?" he asked with a grin.

My eyes lingered upon his face. Perfect white teeth shone as his grin broadened into a crooked smile, which only deepened his dimples and gave him a hint of boyish charm.

A slight rap upon the door drew me from my trance.

"Enter," the pirate announced.

The door opened a crack and the thin face of Mister Smith appeared.

"Beggin' yer pardon, Captain, but might I 'ave a word with ye?" His accented voice much the same as my maid's.

"If you would kindly excuse me, Milady," the Captain said and, rising from his chair, he turned away and walked toward the door.

The men had a brief conversation in hushed whispers and although I strained to hear them, I could only grasp onto a few words, none of which made any sense to me.

"Thank you, Mister Smith. I shall join you on deck momentarily," Captain Drake said, then closed the door and facing me he said, "I must beg your forgiveness, Milady, but if you would kindly excuse me, a matter has arisen which requires my immediate attention."

"Certainly, Captain, but before you go, might I make a request?"

"Milady?"

"I would like to have my maid sent to me, and I truly wish to freshen up a bit. Is there any way I might have a bath?"

"As you wish, Countess," he replied. "Now, if you would kindly excuse me."

He was only gone a moment when Mary appeared at the door.

"Me Lady," she sobbed as she rushed into the room. "I was worried for yer safety. Be ye all right?"

"What did they do to you, Mary? I have been beside myself with worry for you."

"Not to worry. I over'eard the pirates sayin' it be the Captain's orders we was not to be touched."

"Thank heaven."

Despite my maid's obvious anxiety, just having her with me bolstered my resolve.

"Come now, Mary. Compose yourself. Do not fret. I am fine and all will be well. Here, come and sit with me. We'll have a cup of tea."

"Oh, Miss. How can ye be so calm and thinkin' of tea? How is it ye not be afraid? Ye be a brave sort, ye be."

"Who said I am not afraid? I simply refuse to show it." I smiled. "Please, come and sit with me, and we shall plan a strategy to get us through this."

Mary made her way to the table.

"Blimey," she said, "ye must be the bloody guest of honor."

"Whatever makes you say that?"

"The Captain, Miss. Why, he dug out his fine china for ye, he did."

"Mary, it's probably plunder, but you're correct, he perplexes me as well. He seems so out of place. His manner portrays that of a fine gentleman, one born to privilege, yet here he is among this band of miscreants, professing to be a pirate."

"Aye, Miss. He sure 'as an aristocratic air about him and if I may be so bold as to say, he be quite a handsome bloke, wot would be sure to turn any lady's head."

"That he is, Mary, but we must keep our wits about us."

Our conversation was interrupted by a knock on the door. Mary looked at me with wide eyes.

"Do not show them your fear, Mary."

"Wot shall we do?"

"Answer the door just as you would if we were in our home upon the island," I whispered.

"Aye, Miss." She stood and with shaking hands straightened her skirts and made her way to the door. Mister Smith entered, followed by two more men, all of them carrying large, steaming buckets.

"Beggin' yer pardon for the intrusion, yer Ladyship, but the Captain said ye be wantin' to have a bath."

"Yes, Mister Smith, that is true," I answered. After gazing around the room, I asked, "But is there a tub?"

He smiled. "Our Captain, he fancies a bath hisself now 'n again and has a tub here in his quarters," he replied and setting down the buckets of steaming water, he crossed the room to the corner of the cabin where he drew open a thick velvet drape.

My jaw dropped in surprise to see a lovely brass tub set before a floor-to-ceiling mirror. A washstand with a basin stood beside it with thick drying cloths filling its shelves, all in what was a well-appointed bathing chamber, hidden behind the velvet curtain.

The pirates moved quickly to fill the tub and silently made their way from the room.

"Enjoy yer bath yer Ladyship," Mister Smith said, and after casting a quick glance and a wink toward Mary, closed the door silently behind him.

"Why, Mary, I think you have captured Mister Smith's attention."

"I assure ye, Miss, I have done naught to encourage the likes of him."

"Regardless, he seems to have taken a fancy to you nonetheless."

Mary's cheeks turned a bright shade of pink and she cast her gaze toward the floor.

"Do not discount your charms, Mary. In our current situation I fear we may have to use whatever female wiles we possess. Perhaps your wiry Mister Smith will prove to be a valuable ally. Now, if you would kindly assist me, I would like to have my bath while the water is still warm."

Steam rose off the water as I eased myself into the tub. Sitting in the bath was relaxing and, closing my eyes, I rested my head against the back of the rim. It was a luxury I never expected to enjoy while aboard a ship, and I sat there until the kiss of warmth was gone from the water. Finally resigning to the idea of having to get out of the tub, I called for my maid.

"Mary, would you please bring the drying cloth?"

"Aye, Miss. I be right there." She scurried to the side of the tub with an oversized bath towel.

Mary stood before the tub with the large drying cloth spread open. Facing Mary, I reached up to place one hand in hers to steady my balance before stepping from the tub.

"Thank you, Mister Smith. That will be all." My head snapped up at the sound of the dark and dangerous voice, and lifting my gaze over Mary's shoulder, I gasped, and my breath caught in my throat at the sight of Captain Drake standing in the doorway. His crystal green eyes turned dark when he looked at me and despite the fact that the drying cloth was spread before me, heat burned in me from head to toe as his hooded gaze assaulted me.

"I beg your pardon, Milady," he uttered in a hoarse whisper, "I did not realize you were . . ." Following the line of his gaze, I realized he was not looking at my face, but beyond me, over my shoulder. He swallowed hard, and seemed frozen in place, making no move to leave the cabin. The room grew silent but for the sound of my thundering heart and that of his rapid breathing. I turned slowly, anxious to discover what sight had so captured his attention. The loud slamming of the door followed by his footsteps rapidly retreating from the cabin resounded in the room as I stood staring at the sight of my naked body reflected in the full-length mirror behind the tub.

Chapter 5

I didn't know it was possible to blush from head to toe, but the heat that accompanied the flush of embarrassment caused me to lower myself back into the cool water in the tub.

"Come now, Miss. Ye must get yerself out of that cold water and be getting yerself dressed."

"Oh Mary, how will I ever be able to face him again after he has seen my scrawny body?" Just the thought of him having seen me naked brought the sting of heat back to my cheeks.

"Don't ye be thinkin' on it now, Miss. Ye ain't scrawny so don't ye lets me hear ye sayin' that."

"But Father always said I was and he feared he would never make a decent match for me because I was too thin."

"Ye give that no never mind. Ye be a fine an beautiful woman. Ye be a Countess. Need I remind ye of yer station. And that cad o' a Captain dare not be sayin' a word on it either," she replied, helping me step out of the tub to dry off.

"Now, me Lady, we best be gettin' ye dressed."

"I truly wish I had a change of clothes," I said in an attempt to draw my mind away from the look on the Captain's face, which was burned into my memory. Just the thought of it embarrassed me so much it made me wish I could crawl into the nearest hole and die.

"But ye do, Miss. Do ye not be knowin' the Captain had our trunks brought along?"

"He did? I had no idea. Where are they?"

"I believe he had 'em put in the hold."

"I wonder if your Mister Smith would be willing to fetch them for me. Perhaps he would, if you were to ask him."

"Aye, Miss. Let us get ye dressed and presentable and I shall wander out on deck to search for Tobias . . . er . . . I mean, Mister Smith." Color flushed the maid's cheeks.

"Thank you, Mary," I said, suppressing a grin.

After Tobias Smith had the trunks delivered to the cabin, I selected a fresh gown. The deep blue one was one of my favorites, and Mary said this gown accented the best features of my figure and gave a sparkle to my deep blue eyes. Fidgeting in my seat at the dressing table, I watched in the mirror as Mary put my hair up and threaded matching blue ribbon through the curls.

"You seem a bit vexed, Miss," Mary said causally, never taking her hands or eyes from my hair.

"Whatever are you talking about?" Our eyes met in the mirror.

"I don't be meanin' to overstep me place, Miss, but ye be a fidgetin' in this chair like ye did when ye was a mere slip of a girl."

"I'm sorry, Mary. It's just that I-I don't know if I will be able to bring myself to face him."

"A course ye can. Hold yer head up high and . . ."

A sharp rapping on the door interrupted her. She took a step to answer it, but I grabbed her arm.

"No, Mary. Please do not open that door."

"But, Miss."

An impatient knock sounded again, and Mary took another step closer.

"Mary, please," I begged, "I'm not ready."

"Aye, ye be ready, Miss." Turning, she walked the few steps to the door and opened it. Mister Smith hurried in carrying a large tray, which appeared to weigh more than he did. He placed it down on the table, and I stood to face him.

"Thank you, Mister Smith."

"The Captain will be here directly to dine," he muttered as he scampered toward the door.

"Mister Smith," I said, raising my voice more than I'd intended.

He turned, and, shifting his weight from one foot to the other, replied, "Aye, yer Ladyship?"

His glance danced between me and Mary. My mouth got dry at the thought that he might know the Captain had walked in on my bath, and I could not bring myself to look him in the eye. Gathering my courage, I lifted my chin a notch and mustered what I hoped was a stern glare.

"Please notify Captain Drake that I do not wish to dine with him. I shall take my evening meal here with Mary, and I ask that he kindly take his with the crew."

"Aye, yer Ladyship. I'll be sure to relay yer message to the Captain." And again, he chanced a glance toward Mary, then added, "But he won't be happy."

"His happiness is of no concern to me. Thank you, Mister Smith, that will be all."

"Aye, yer Ladyship," he said, and as he backed out of the cabin his gaze shifted again to the maid.

As soon as the door closed behind him, I turned to my maid.

"Mary, what is going on between you and Smith?"

"I don't be knowin' what ye be talkin' about. There be nothin' goin' on, Miss."

"Mary, do not lie to me. Were you planning to take your evening meal with Mister Smith?"

"Aye, Miss," she replied, wringing her hands as she cast her eyes toward the floor.

"Very well, Mary. I do not wish to spoil your plans. You go ahead. It's just that I do not wish to dine with . . . with *him*."

"Thank ye, Miss." Mary bobbed a quick courtesy and scurried toward the door.

"Mary!"

"Aye, Miss?" The timid maid turned back to face me.

"Enjoy your dinner." I smiled.

"Thank ye, Miss," she said and rushed out the cabin as if she feared I might change my mind.

The delicious aroma of food floated across the room like an enticing, unseen hand drawing me toward it and causing my stomach to rumble. I could not recall the last time I had eaten and I made my way to the table, nearly floating on the delicious smells.

The tray was laden with plates, each containing something different. There were platters filled with exotic fruits and nuts, some with roasted potatoes, others had vegetables, breads, roasted meats, and delicate cakes. A feast for the eyes as well as the stomach, and one certainly fit for a king. My mouth watered as I took a plate and began to fill it with delectable morsels. Taking a seat at the vast table and picking up a fork, I stabbed a slice of rare beef.

The fork was nearly halfway to my mouth when the door to the cabin flew open with such force it slammed into the wall. I jumped from my seat, dropping the fork in the process.

He stood there in the doorway, his eyes dark and dangerous and his hands balled into fists at his sides. His breath came in quick rasps and he closed his eyes for a moment, clearly fighting to rein in his anger. When his eyes finally opened they were still dark, but his expression seemed to have softened somewhat.

"Captain," I said in a meek voice, "is something amiss?"

"Aye, Milady. At the end of a very long day, I wish for the solitude of my cabin and the comfort of a warm meal."

He took a few steps into the cabin and closing the door behind him made his way to the table. Picking up a plate, he began to make a few selections from the tray. I stood there watching him, and the slow burn of anger spread through me. *How dare he ignore my wishes!*

When he had filled his plate to his satisfaction, he took the seat across from mine at the table. Standing there with my arms crossed, I glared at him.

"Would you care for some wine, Milady?" he asked, pouring the dark red liquid into the silver goblets.

"No, I would not care for any wine. What I would like is to be left alone to enjoy my evening meal in solitude."

"Is this not my cabin?" he asked with a raised eyebrow, his gaze surveying the room.

"Yes."

"I thought as much. My cabin is where I customarily take my meals."

"Did Mister Smith not deliver my message?"

"Aye, I received your message."

"Yet you chose to ignore my wishes?"

"Need I remind you, Countess, despite the fact that you are being treated with respect and dignity, you are, in fact, my prisoner?"

Temper bubbled up from somewhere deep inside me and before I realized it, the silver goblet was in my hand. Tossing its content in his face, I flung the empty goblet aside and strode toward the door.

"Enjoy your meal, Captain," I said, storming from the room.

Chapter 6

The night air was cool and refreshing against the heat of my cheeks. I rushed along the deck until I found myself breathless and standing at the prow of the vessel. Closing my eyes, I allowed the peacefulness of the rise and fall of the ship cutting through the sea to ease my ire. *I refuse to allow that man to bait me or best me. Surely if he were to harm me in any way, it would render me worthless, and he would have no claim to a ransom. Nay, he shall not harm me. I refuse to cow down to his demands. We shall see who really is in control aboard this ship.* Once I came up with this strategy, my temper began to cool.

My hand rested on the smooth wood of the rail while I watched the moonlight dance upon the waves, the sound of the wind in the sails was almost liberating. I don't know how long he stood behind me in silence but when I sensed his presence, my backbone stiffened. *What was it about this man that riled me so?*

He took a few steps closer. "Catherine," he said in a voice just above a whisper. The deepness of his murmur caused my mind to wander. *Why was I picturing him using this tone with a lover?* My back stiffened further and I chided myself for allowing my thoughts to wander in that direction. Refusing to face him, I kept my gaze upon the water.

"It would give me great pleasure if you would do me the honor of dining with me this evening." He seemed to purr.

He inched closer and the heat of his body radiated into

my rigid back. Placing one hand upon my shoulder and his lips close to my ear he whispered, "Please."

The heat of his whisper caressed my ear and the tension seemed to melt away from me. I closed my eyes and tried to swallow the lump in my throat.

"You look truly beautiful this evening, Milady." His hoarse whisper scorched my neck and goose bumps ran up my arms. He stood so close that when I relaxed, my back nestled against his chest. His body was hard and warm and the intoxicating smell of him made me dizzy. Heat spread through me in a sensation I had never experienced before as his soft lips gently brushed my neck, but my heart nearly stopped when he whispered, "But not nearly as lovely as you looked this afternoon in the mirror."

Chapter 7

I tried to pull away from him, but he tightened his hold on my arm. He turned me to face him and the look in his deep green eyes disarmed me. They were still dark, but seemed to soften somehow, almost pleading. I couldn't draw my gaze from his, and my heart fluttered as he drew me further into his embrace. His arms wrapped around me and despite his size and strength, he held me gently.

The moonlight reflecting off the water gleamed in his hooded eyes and the gentle breeze dancing around us gave me the feeling of being caught up in a hypnotic and magical dream. A warm heat spread through me, seeping into my bones. I was surprised when, almost against my will, I leaned into him. His body was muscular and hard, yet at the same time, warm and inviting. He drew me closer, and I rested my head upon his chest. His heart raced beneath my ear when he buried his face in my hair. A deep, contented sigh came from somewhere, and I was shocked to realize it had come from me. When he drew his lips away from my hair, I instinctively lifted my face to look up at him. Slowly he leaned toward me, his eyes dark and smoldering.

His full lips were soft as he placed them against mine and unable to help myself, I responded to him. A low moan escaped him and seemed to give me the courage not to pull away. *Father would surely disapprove of this, and I certainly should not encourage this inappropriate behavior.* My mind raced, trying hard to grasp onto rational thought.

I wound my arms around his neck and he ran one hand up my back, deepening his kiss. I felt dizzy as a warm tingling feeling rushed through me. His lips parted slightly and when he ran the tip of his tongue over my lips, a bolt of energy surged through me like liquid lightening, and I gasped. When I did, my lips parted slightly and I thought I would burst with the feeling that came over me when his tongue began to slowly explore the depths of my mouth. *How could anything that felt so pleasant be looked upon as inappropriate?*

Unsure of what to do, or what my response should be, I followed his lead and as my tongue danced with his, a deep moan escaped him and his breathing became rapid. His slow kiss continued, then he drew one hand up along my ribs to my breast. His fingers caressed me gently and a rush of wet heat flooded the center of my womanhood. This time the moan came from me.

His kiss deepened. He ran his hand down my spine and, cupping my bottom, pressed me against him. I instantly became aware of the hardness of him and alarms suddenly sounded in my mind, yet I was unable to force myself to pull away from him. The feelings he stirred in me were like drinking a deep red wine, and I clung to him, drunk with it and wanting more. My fingers wound through his hair, and the ribbon holding his raven locks fell away.

"Catherine," he whispered into his kiss.

My hands explored his hard muscular chest. I was eager and addicted to this new excitement he ignited in me. Abruptly, he pulled away from me. He stood there with his eyes closed and body shaking. I was stunned. *Had I done something wrong?*

My mouth burned from his kiss, and I raised my fingers to touch my swollen lips. Heat surged through me. Puzzled, I watched him, standing before me, struggling, and clearly fighting with himself.

Finally, he opened his eyes and in a hoarse whisper, he managed to utter, "Milady, please, forgive me."

"Forgive you?"

"Aye, and kindly excuse me, for if I do not depart from you at this very moment, I fear I shall not be able to drag myself away," he said and turning, he walked away from me and into the darkness.

Chapter 8

He did not come to his cabin that night, as I had feared he would, and for that I was thankful. But the scent of him clung to the bed linens and I tossed and turned with thoughts of our encounter playing over and over in my mind. Finally, the light of dawn filtered into the cabin and unable to tolerate this restlessness a moment longer, I got up and dressed myself. I selected the floral print gown because it laced up the front and I was able to get into it without Mary's assistance. The sun still hung low on the horizon when I made my way up to the main deck.

"'Mornin', yer Ladyship," Smith said.

"Good morning, Mister Smith. Have you seen Captain Drake?"

"Aye, he be at the wheel, but I'd give him a wide berth today, yer Ladyship. He be in a right foul mood."

"I see. I shall take heed to your warning."

"I wasn't prepared for ye to be up an' about so early, but I be gettin' yer breakfast brung to yer cabin directly, yer Ladyship."

"Thank you, Mister Smith, but would it be possible to take my breakfast up here in the fresh air?"

"Aye, Miss. As ye wish," he answered and scampered away.

I strolled casually along the deck, fighting the urge to look toward the wheel. The pirate crew moved about with purpose in their work and for the most part, ignored me. I walked mindlessly until I found myself standing again at the prow. Leaning against the rail, I closed my eyes and allowed the sea breeze to wash over me, the salty mist cool upon my face. Standing there, the thoughts of my encounter with Edmund played through my mind and a warm sensation filled me.

I jumped at the sound of a rough voice. "'Mornin', yer Ladyship," the scruffy Mister Taylor said.

A twinge of fear coupled with revulsion gripped me and, swallowing hard, I managed to mutter, "Good day, Mister Taylor."

"Ye be a picture a loveliness this mornin', me Lady."

"Thank you," I replied, holding myself tall and giving him what I considered to be my most authoritative glare.

"But not nearly the vision ye be last night," he whispered, drawing up close to me. Shock must have been written on my face, because he saw fit to explain his statement.

"Aye, I saw ye in his arms, allowin' 'im liberties." He grabbed me, pulling me close to his rank body.

"Take your hands off of me!" I demanded and struggled to pull away from him, but his grip was strong as he dragged me back away from the rail.

"Nay, me Lady. I be plannin' ta enjoy some of what ye seemed ta be givin' so freely ta the Captain last night."

"I gave nothing to the Captain nor do I have any intention of allowing you—"

"I takes wot I wants."

My heart thundered in my ears and my knees shook.

"What do you think Captain Drake would do to you if you bring me to ruin? He would never be able to demand his ransom."

"I ain't gunna tell 'im an wot he don't know ain't gunna hurt none."

He leaned in to kiss me, and I turned away just in time. His slobbering wet kiss landing upon my cheek made my stomach roll. Shoving him away from me, my hand flew up and I slapped him across the face with all my might. He merely laughed.

"Ye li'l minx. So, ye likes it rough now, does ye? I can give it to ye rough," he hissed, slamming me up against the base of the mast.

He thrust himself against me, and when he pressed his thin lips to mine, bile rose in my throat. I tried to scream, but his disgusting kiss swallowed the sound. Pushing and punching at him did no good and only seemed to increase his vigor. He was like a demon possessed. He pawed roughly at my breast, and as he began to unfasten his britches, panic gripped me. My entire body shook with fear and I closed my eyes as tight as I could, trying to shut the entire scene out.

The next thing I knew, the weight of Mister Taylor's foul body was no longer against me. My eyes flew opened to see Captain Drake holding Mister Taylor up by the shirtfront. The vile pirate's feet were raised off the deck by a good measure. The two men were eye-to-eye with mere inches between their faces.

"Mister Taylor, I believe the Lady asked you to take your hands off of her," Edmund said through gritted teeth. His deep voice dripped with the threat of danger and despite myself, my body tingled with the excitement of that danger.

I smoothed my dress back into place with trembling hands. Dizziness overcame me. Even my legs shook, and I leaned against the mast for fear I might swoon.

"Aye, Captain."

"I suggest you keep your distance from the Countess, Mister Taylor."

The filthy ruffian glared at me. "This ain't over, Missy. Ye best not let me be findin' ye alone again, lest I finish what be started," he growled.

"Is that a threat, Mister Taylor?" the Captain bellowed. Silence.

His eyes grew dark and anger flashed behind them as he continued, "I suggest you spend your energies on your duties and stay away from the Countess, for if I see you even spare her a glance, you will find yourself spending the remainder of this voyage in the brig. Is that clear?"

"Aye, Captain, but she ain't seen the last o' this." Taylor said with hate-filled eyes.

The commotion drew other crew members who now stood around us waiting to see what their Captain's next move would be.

Edmund's eyes scanned the crowd. "Mister Smith," he said, releasing the scruffy Mister Taylor, who fell to the deck with a thud.

"Aye, Captain," the Quartermaster called out, weaving his way through the crowd.

"Take Mister Taylor to the brig."

"The brig? But, but I thought ye said . . ." Mister Taylor stammered, scrambling to his feet.

"Yes, the brig and that's where you shall remain until you learn that my orders are to be followed. I will not tolerate insubordination. Is that clear?"

The air grew thick with tension. A low grumble passed through the crew like a wave.

Mister Smith grabbed Taylor by the scruff of the neck and shoved him along the deck ahead him. "Off ye go, Taylor. Ye knows the way."

"Aye," Taylor muttered and the scruffy pirate slithered away with Mister Smith following close behind him.

When the Captain turned to me, his eyes still dark and dangerous, my breath caught in my throat.

"Countess, need I remind you of my warning not to venture away from my side. There is danger in wandering about this ship unaccompanied." A muscle twitched in his lean cheek.

"And what of the danger in staying by your side, Captain?"

"I apologize for my behavior of last night, my dear Countess, and trust me when I say I shall endeavor to do my best to see that it does not happen again." He abruptly turned and stormed away, nearly bumping into Mary who ran toward me.

"Miss, wot on earth has ye up at such an early hour? Come now, breakfast be waitin'."

I found I couldn't speak. I watched Edmund's retreating back. *We shall see, my good Captain . . . we shall see.*

Chapter 9

The ship was huge, with three masts all boasting great square white sails. It had become a favorite pastime of mine to watch the men sing as they worked together to raise and lower those beautiful sails. The chanteys they sang were quite funny and some I admit a bit saucy. The grand ship was taller than any building I had ever seen, and I was certain anyone who should happen to fall overboard would surely meet his death. Yet men would climb the rigging with no fear. The cabin boy, Jake, was particularly nimble at it, and could climb more quickly than the others, even with a bucket and brush in hand. Often times I watched him walk across the mast beam with the ease of a man walking upon the deck, and once I saw him swing on a rope all the way down to the deck.

Having been aboard the ship for some time now, I was becoming bored and longed for the freedom of being up there like Jake, to be able to scan the horizon for miles. One day I asked him if he would teach me to climb the rigging.

"Oh, me Lady, I would have to seek the permission of the Captain. Aside from that, ye cannot be climbin' up them ropes in no fancy gown."

"Jake, we look to be about the same size. If you were to loan me a pair of britches and a shirt, then we could climb together."

"I don't be thinkin' that to be such a good idea, me Lady. The Captain, he be sure to disapprove."

"You let me worry about the Captain."

"I suppose then, if it be okay with the Captain, I could."

"When?"

"Whenever ye like."

"Now. I want to do it today. Hurry, Jake, and get me something appropriate to wear. I shall meet you outside my cabin."

"Aye, me Lady. You speak on it with the Captain, and I'll get ye some britches," he said. I smiled as he rushed off toward the crews' quarters.

Before long, I stood upon the deck wearing britches and a man's shirt, with my hair in a long braid.

"Now, me Lady, first I be tyin' this here line around ye," he began.

"Why? Why do I need one when you do not wear one?"

"I been climbin' the riggin' all me life. This line will save ye from death should ye fall."

"All right then, I suppose it is necessary."

"Now, me Lady, I'll be right beside ye. Watch what I be doin' and do the like."

It was harder than I expected, but since I was fit from caring for the horses and stables, it wasn't long before I had climbed halfway to the top. The thick ropes of the rigging were rough under my bare feet but the view was amazing. As I gazed out to the horizon, I could see for miles. The sea glistened ahead of us and I thought I spied a scrap of land, but could not be certain. *Was there more beyond the tiny island?* If only I could climb higher, I would know for sure. I could only imagine what the view from the top could be like.

"Jake, I want to climb to the top."

"Nay, me Lady. The rope ye be wearin' ain't secured high enough for ye to climb that far."

"Then we shall simply do without the rope."

"Nay, I cannot allow that. The Captain will kill me if ye should meet your death."

"Jake, who is that up there beside you?" a voice boomed from below.

I peered down to see the Captain standing below us on the deck. But my gaze traveled beyond him to the water so very far below. Dizziness swirled around my head, and everything started to spin. I gasped for breath and grabbed hold of the rigging, holding on as tightly as I could.

"Ye be all right, me Lady?" Jake asked.

I couldn't answer him . . . I could hardly breathe.

"Jake! You best not tell me that is the Countess up there with you," the Captain yelled.

"Aye, Captain," Jake yelled back.

The humming in my ears became deafening and my grasp upon the ropes of the rigging tightened to the point my knuckles grew white. My palms began to sweat and I feared I would lose my grip.

"Get her down from there immediately!" the Captain ordered.

"Captain, I don't be thinkin' she can move," Jake called back.

Jake placed his hand softly upon my shoulder and said, "Countess, do ye think ye can climb down?"

I stared straight ahead, seeing nothing, and it took all my strength to whisper, "I don't know."

"Try. Try to move yer foot. Bring one foot down to the rope beneath ye."

But no matter how hard I concentrated, I could not force myself to move.

"I can't Jake. I-I'm . . ." I couldn't bring myself to say I was afraid.

"Jake, what the devil is going on up there?" the Captain called.

I flinched as the pirate's ire only added to my anxiety.

"Give me a minute, Captain," the boy replied. Turning

to me, he said, "Me Lady, don't look down . . . look at me . . . look to me eyes."

I forced myself to face him, staring into Jake's soft brown eyes.

"Good . . . now, we be goin' to climb down the riggin' . . . together. That be all right?"

My breath sounded like thunder, sweat trickled down my back, and my limbs were shaking. I couldn't even answer him.

"Jake, I'm coming up," the Captain yelled.

I closed my eyes, trying to gain some courage, but found that to be a mistake for then I couldn't force myself to open them again. I kept my eyes closed as tight as I could and tried to focus on breathing. *Why did going up not bring so much as a glimmer of fear, while looking down from where I came threatens to send me over the edge of panic?*

"Milady." Edmund's voice was a whisper against my ear. "I'm here and I'm going to take you down. We're going to do this together. I vow to you, I shall not allow you to fall."

It was then I felt the warmth of his body seeping into me as he drew himself up behind me.

"Lean back. We shall move as one." He put one hand over mine upon the ropes. Still, I couldn't force myself to move.

"Catherine," he whispered against my ear, "trust me." Placing his arm around my waist, he drew my body against his. His arm around me felt like an iron band and from somewhere deep inside, I managed to gather a small measure of courage and loosened my grip upon the rope. My breathing was still raspy, but closer to normal as we slowly began descending, moving together, and all the while he whispered soft encouragements in my ear.

Finally, I felt the solid deck beneath my feet. Turning me to face him, he placed his fingers beneath my chin and lifted my face to look at him. "Catherine, you must give me your word that you will never do anything so foolhardy again."

Shame flooded me, but he held my face between his hands and I could not turn away from him. I looked down at the deck as tears streamed down my cheeks.

"No need to cry," he whispered, and drew me closer into his embrace.

Still unable to find my voice, my tears soaked into his shirt. He stood there patiently allowing me the time to gather my composure.

When I was able to find my voice, I stepped slightly away from him and said, "Thank you, Captain, for rescuing me." I still could not meet his gaze.

"Catherine, you gave me quite a fright."

"I'm sorry."

"No need for apologies, Milady, but there is a need for you to change your clothes. I shall not be able to rescue you from my crew should they catch sight of your shapely derrière in those britches. I must admit, Madam, I find my own resolve to be sorely tested."

Chapter 10

The days slipped by and although the Captain kept his distance, I was never out of his sight. However, every time I chanced a glance at him, it seemed his scowl deepened, and the crew openly complained of his bad temper. One morning while walking on deck with Mary, I overheard two of the pirates talking.

"It be 'er wot got the Captain in such a temper."

"The Countess?"

"Aye. The sooner we gets 'er off this ship, the better. Women aboard ship be bad luck."

"For a piece o' bad luck, she sure be a right pretty one."

"Aye, that she be."

"Maybe that be what vexes the Captain. Maybe he's taken a fancy to her."

"Nay, he wouldn't have."

"Aye, watch 'ow he looks at her."

Suddenly the two sailors became aware of the fact that their conversation was no longer private and looked nervously at each other as I approached.

"Good day, Gentlemen," I said with a smile, hoping to not indicate I had overheard their conversation.

"Me Lady," they replied in unison.

Strolling along past them, I lowered my voice to a whisper and asked, "Mary, do you think there is any merit to what the pirates said just then?"

"Oh, Miss, I couldn't say."

"You know, I have never met a man like Captain Drake."

"Ye ain't never 'ad the chance to meet many men on the island. But bein' a Lady, ye ain't really acquainted overmuch with the ways o' men. As well ye shouldn't be."

"No, but still the Captain is nothing like my father."

"No Miss, I don't suppose he is. Yer father is a gent, he is, an' well, the Captain, he be a pirate."

The sound of her words faded as the memory of my father's cowardice the day we were taken brought a fresh sting of pain to my heart. He never even spoke a word to try and save me. Was I such a burden to him that he would so easily allow me to be taken? Despite the pain the memory of that day brought me, I couldn't help but wonder what had become of him and the crew of *The Tempest*.

I sighed. Forcing the memory of my father's drawn face from my mind I walked along with Mary in silence. We strolled together past the pirates engaged in their duties. They hardly spared us a glance, yet the smell of their dirty clothes and filthy bodies nearly choked me. Then the seed of a thought sprouted in my mind.

"Mary, today we shall make some well-needed changes aboard this ship."

"Oh, now, Miss, don't ye be causin' no more of a fuss. What ye be plannin' to do this time?"

"Well, to start with, these men are all in dire need of a bath."

"Oh, Miss." She giggled. "They won't likely be takin' kindly to that I wager."

"I care little for how they will be taking to it, but it is necessary. I have had animals that have smelled far better than most of these men."

"Aye, Miss. That be true."

"It will be necessary to enlist the aid of your Mister Smith. Do you think you have enough influence over him to coax him to help us?"

"I'll give it me best try."

Later that afternoon, Mister Smith and a few crew members dragged the big brass tub from the Captain's cabin up to the deck. Each crew member was instructed to bathe and wash their clothes. Shirts and britches hung on the rails and in the rigging drying in the wind as the last of the pirate crew lined up for a bath. Their grumbling was short lived when I arrived. "Gentlemen, it is now a pleasure to stand among you. Who would have ever imagined such handsome men to be hidden beneath all that grime?" I walked between them, straightening a collar here and there, and touching a clean-shaven face.

Their smiles told me the flattery had hit its mark.

"What the devil is going on here?" the Captain's deep voice boomed from behind me.

Mister Smith was quick to reply.

"Beggin' yer pardon, Captain, Sir, but I thought it be fittin', since we have a Lady aboard, that the men make themselves more presentable. Clean themselves up a bit . . . it be only right."

His eyes traveled over the clothes hanging in the rigging and along the rails, and he shook his head. Walking to stand before me, he asked, "The crew is wearing their Sunday best, are they? Is this your doing, Countess?"

"Nay, Captain," Smith quickly answered, "it be mine."

"Would you care for a bath, Captain?" I teased.

Looking down at me, his eyes danced with amusement. Leaning closer, he whispered so only I could hear, "Is that an invitation, Milady? Would you care to wash my back?"

My cheeks burned. Part of me wanted to slap him and part of me wanted to watch the trails of warm soapy water run down his strong, naked back.

That night, as in keeping with my new strategy, I decided Mary and I would take our evening meal with the crew. As we made our way along the dark and narrow passageway to the galley, butterflies danced in my stomach at the prospects of seeing *him*.

Laughter and the sounds of conversation and genuine camaraderie emanated from the galley, but as soon as I entered the room, the men's voices fell silent. My eyes roamed the galley. The dark wooden table seemed to take up the entire room. Lanterns hung from the low ceiling casting their glow about the room. Great platters of food were laid out upon the table. My gaze fell upon the faces of each crew member. Their blank expressions made me self-conscious. I quickly scanned the crowd, looking for Edmund, but he was not present. Struggling to hide my disappointment, I said, "Good evening, gentlemen. Please, please continue with your conversation."

Wide-eyed stares accompanied by gaping looks of astonishment made up their reply.

"Gentlemen, I hope you do not mind if I take my evening meal with you," I said with the hint of a question.

"Nay, me Lady," Tobias Smith answered, jumping up to offer me his seat. Mary sat in the seat beside me to my right.

"Thank you, Mister Smith. As I approached the galley, it sounded as if you were engaged in lively conversation. Please do not allow me to interrupt."

An awkward silence resounded.

As I filled my plate, I attempted a casual conversation.

"I would like to thank you gentlemen once again for bathing today."

Silence.

"I truly appreciate your efforts and cooperation."

More silence.

"I thought I would mention that I have discovered some very interesting tomes in the Captain's cabin, and I wonder if any of you would be interested in hearing me read aloud."

Some shook their heads in agreement, but still remained silent.

"What the devil is this?" *His* voice boomed over the silence.

"Good evening, Captain." I spun toward him and graced him with what I thought to be my most alluring smile.

"Good evening, Countess," he replied in a tone which held a tinge of annoyance. A deep frown creased his brow.

"Would you care to join us?" I asked.

"No, thank you, Milady. Mister Smith, please see that a plate is brought up to me. I shall be at the wheel."

"Aye, Captain," Smith answered.

"Are you certain, Captain? There is plenty of room. Here, you may sit next to me." I patted the seat of the empty chair beside me to my left.

"That's very kind of you, Countess, but my attention is required elsewhere."

"Pity. We shall miss your company." I smiled again.

His eyes grew dark, and my pulse raced when danger flashed behind his gaze.

"Yes, quite," he replied, then strode from the galley.

After the dinner plates were cleared from the table, the cook brought a heaping plate of succulent meat and roasted vegetables and potatoes and handed it to Mister Smith.

"Mister Smith, I would be happy to deliver that plate of food up to the Captain," I said to the wiry quartermaster who stood there with the Captain's dinner plate in his hand.

"Me Lady . . . I . . ."

Taking the plate from his hands, I strode from the galley, leaving him standing open-mouthed behind me.

Climbing the steps to the upper deck, I found Edmund standing at the wheel staring out into the night.

"Captain?"

"Yes, Countess, how can I help you this evening?" He turned to face me as I approached him.

The breeze tousled his hair and brought his manly scent directly to me, stirring emotions in me I didn't know existed. I paused momentarily to compose myself before I replied.

"I have brought your dinner up to you. Where would you like me to place it?"

"There on that chest behind you. Thank you."

"You're welcome."

He drew his gaze away from me and stared out again into the night. When I didn't move to leave, he faced me again and asked, "What is it, Countess?"

"How do you know where you're going?"

He chuckled. "Here, come stand before the wheel."

He stepped aside and motioned for me to come and stand between him and the great wooden wheel. I did as he requested.

"Place your hands upon the wheel, here upon the handles," he said, indicating the location by tapping the spokes. When I placed my hands upon the smooth palm-sized handles, I found the heat of his grip still clung to them.

I turned to ask him questions, but he moved to stand closer to me, nearly pressing his chest against my back. I held my breath, waiting. He stood so close I felt the heat of him seeping into my back, but excitement filled me when he placed his hands over mine upon the wheel. His arms rested against mine and his chest nestled against my back. He leaned close to me and whispered in my ear, "Relax, Catherine. Do you feel the movement of the ship?"

"Yes," I whispered, "but how do you know your direction in the dark of night?"

"By the stars." He stepped even closer, and my head rested against his shoulder.

"Do you know any of the constellations?"

"No . . . I . . ." Suddenly I felt embarrassed by the lack of a proper education. "I fear there are many things I do not have the knowledge of."

His chuckle rumbled against my back. "Very well, then there are many things I shall have to teach you." His warm breath brushed against my ear, and a shiver rushed through me.

"You are chilled, Milady?" He planted a trail of warm kisses along my neck. "Allow me to warm you."

"Captain, I . . ."

He turned me in his arms, and drew me into his embrace. I gazed up into his eyes, and knew I could easily drown in the depths of those deep green pools. He lowered his warm lips to meet mine. His kiss was tender and sweet, and held a promise, a promise I sensed but could not understand. My arms wound around his neck. I craved more, and he gave me what I craved. His lips took mine in a deep kiss. His tongue invaded the depths of my mouth and began a slow, sensual dance with mine. His fingers pulled the comb from my hair, allowing my curls to tumble down my back, and he drew his fingers through the silky length.

Drawing his lips away from mine, he held me gently in his arms burying his face in my hair. He trembled in my arms, and warm heat pooled in the center of my womanhood. I didn't know what caused him to struggle so, but I knew I didn't want him to stop kissing me. His lips caressed mine once more and I sighed into our kiss.

His hand rose to caress my breast, and a soft moan escaped my lips. I was in deep water, and I was drowning in a sea of desire. I was torn, wanting him to continue, but, even in my ignorance, knowing I should not allow it.

His warm fingers slipped beneath the bodice of my gown, then beneath my chemise. I placed my hand upon his in an effort to stop him, but when his fingers stroked my nipple, a flood of pleasure ran through me. I never dreamed such exquisite sensations were possible.

I could no longer think, could no longer reason. I knew this was wrong, but it felt so right. I wanted to feel his hands on my skin. There in the dark, with only the stars as our witness, I wanted him to touch me, and I wanted to touch him. I was not even conscious that I had unbuttoned his shirt, until I felt the warmth of his naked chest beneath my palm. I had no idea what to do other than to mimic his actions. Finding his nipple, I allowed my fingertips to make gentle circles over it. A soft moan came from his throat.

He drew his lips from mine, his breathing ragged, his eyes hooded, filled with a dangerous look.

Thinking I had done something wrong, my fingers stilled, and rested over his heart, which thundered beneath my touch.

He placed his warm hand upon mine. Heat raged through me and my stomach tightened. Taking my hand in his, he gently guided my fingers to touch the bulge at the front of his trousers. Fear prickled my spine, and I pulled my hand away. He gently guided my touch back to the hard bulge. "This is what you do to me, Catherine," he murmured. "I want you. I have tried to stay away from you, but I find I cannot help myself."

"Edmund, I-I never . . ." His kiss blocked my words. Still, I could not bring myself to keep my hand there upon his hardness. Not knowing what to do, I wound my arms around his neck.

His lips captured mine, and in the heat of desire, I had not realized he had lifted my breast free from my gown. He lowered his head, leaving a trail of hot kisses that sent a shot of hot wetness between my legs. His lips touched my nipple and he gently sucked my sensitive flesh into the depths of his warm mouth.

My head rolled back and I clung to him as pleasure ripped through me. He held me to him, rolling my nipple around with his tongue.

I felt the coolness of the night against my skin, but it did not cool the fire of desire burning in my soul.

He drew the skirt of my gown upward. I knew I was venturing into dangerous waters, but I couldn't stop myself. I didn't want to. It felt sinful, and totally wicked, but I wanted him to touch me. His hand ran up my inner thigh, and I groaned.

My flesh burned beneath his touch as he traced a slow warm trail up my thigh. The tips of his fingers brushed aside my undergarment and grazed the soft hair nestled between my legs, and I moaned in anticipation.

"Captain, ye 'bout done wit yer dinner?" Mister Smith called as he started up the steps toward the wheel deck.

"Edmund," I whispered. I didn't want to be caught in this compromising situation, yet I didn't want him to stop. Waves of disappointment washed over me when I felt the weight of my skirt fall back to the floor as Edmund released me. He moved quickly to adjust the bodice of my gown and cover my nakedness. I turned away from him and faced the great wheel, my breathing still raspy from our encounter.

"Oh, sorry, Captain . . . I didn't realize . . . I . . . ." Smith stammered as he averted his gaze.

"No, no, Mister Smith. I was instructing the Countess on reading the stars and teaching her how to handle the wheel."

"Aye, I'm sure ye was teachin' her 'ow te handle somethin'," he murmured under his breath. He inclined his head toward me and said, "Evenin', Countess."

"Good evening, Mister Smith," I uttered, thankful for the moonless night that hid my embarrassment. *How had I allowed this to go so far? Allowed myself to get so carried away?*

"I see ye ain't touched yer dinner, Captain."

"Nay, as I said, Mister Smith, I was instructing the Countess."

"Guess ye ain't hungry then?"

"Oh, yes, Mister Smith . . . I'm hungry."

"Aye, I be sure ye be. Ye want me te leave the plate then?"

"Aye."

"I'll leave ye then to yer lesson." He turned to retreat.

"No, wait, Mister Smith. I believe the Captain has finished with the lesson, and I should probably get to my cabin." Then looking to Edmund, I continued. "Thank you, Captain, for the insightful education."

"It was a pleasure, Countess. I look forward to your next lesson."

I rushed past Mister Smith and made my way down to my cabin, praying no one noticed the color that I knew must be staining my cheeks.

Chapter 11

That night I tossed and turned in the oversized bed, as memories of his kisses haunted my dreams. Visions of him sitting naked in a tub of warm bath water left me breathless. As I tossed and turned, my legs became entwined in the bed linens, causing me to dream of Edmund. Imagining his warm lips roaming my body, his tongue licking my nipples as he did at the wheel, his fingers running up my thighs caused a hot flood of desire to pool in my core.

I sat bolt upright in bed, panting for breath. In my fitful sleep, I thought I heard the sound of the cabin door closing. Yet when I lit the candle and surveyed the room, I found no one to be there.

The following morning, Mary and I strolled along the deck together. I had planned to begin reading to the crew, but as I walked along a thought occurred to me. I could use this opportunity to my advantage, if I choose to sit in precisely the right place. Coming across a small stack of crates, directly in the Captain's line-of-sight, I smiled. *Perfect.*

"Here. We shall sit here, Mary," I announced.

Following the line of my gaze, Mary whispered, "I fear ye be playin' with fire by tauntin' the Captain so, Miss."

"Far better this than a life spent in a loveless marriage with the Old Duke."

Straightening my skirts, I sat upon the crate and mustering what I thought to be my most innocent look, I opened the book, a leather-bound tomb containing tales written by Homer. Six or seven men drew closer, but no one wanted to be the first to approach.

"Come, gentlemen, sit here upon the deck," I said, indicating the space at my feet, "and I shall begin." I gave them my most dazzling smile.

Mister Smith stood at the back of the group. I was uncertain as to the reason for his interest, the reading or my maid, but I said nothing.

Clearing my throat and lifting the book, I began to read. As my eyes skimmed over the words, I was eager to steal a glance toward the man who stood at the wheel, but dared not.

My voice sounded clear and strong as I read and interest shown upon the men's faces as the tale of Odysseus unfolded. I wondered if anyone had ever read to any of the men since their childhood, or even if then.

More engrossed in the telling of the tale, the thoughts of chancing a peek at the Captain slipped to the back of my mind. The feeling of his dark stare burned into me, and I began to fidget in my seat. Finally unable to tolerate it a moment longer, I gave in to my curiosity and lifted my eyes to glance toward him. My gaze was met by clear green eyes dancing with amusement. My heart skipped a beat and my breath caught in my throat as his eyes darkened and he drew his gaze away from mine.

I glanced at Mister Smith, who had followed the line of my stare and witnessed the exchange. Hardly able to find my voice, I lowered my eyes back to the volume in my trembling hand but found it impossible to resume reading.

"That will be all for today. My voice grows tired," I murmured, much to my audience's disapproval.

"You heard the Countess," Smith chimed. "Besides, it be well past the time ye be gettin' to work. Move along now, move along."

"I shall read more tomorrow, I promise," I said. *But next time I shall find a place out of* his *line-of-sight.*

"Thank you, Mister Smith."

"It weren't nothin', me Lady," he answered, and turned to walk away.

"Mister Smith?"

"Aye."

"Come, sit with me a moment."

The wiry man chanced a quick glance up toward the Captain, but complied with my request and sat upon a crate next to me.

"Wot can I do for ye?"

"Mister Smith, I would like to teach you to speak as a gentleman."

"A gent, ye say?"

"Yes, Mister Smith, a gentleman. Now, repeat after me. How do you do?"

"'ow doo ye doo?"

"No, no, no. It's not 'oow doo ye doo' . . . it is 'how do you do?'"

"Aye, me Lady, that be wot I said."

I fought to control the twitch of my lips upward. After all, he was trying.

"Mister Smith, when you meet another gentleman you must say 'I am pleased to make your acquaintance.' Now, you try it."

"I be pleased te be makin' yer acquaintance."

"I am. Not I be."

"I am pleased te be makin' yer acquaintance." He smiled with pride.

"That's better, but we must practice."

"Aye . . . er . . . yes, that be true."

I frowned.

"Yes, tis true?" He smiled.

"Very good, Mister Smith."

"Do ye really be thinkin' ye can teach me to be a proper gent?"

"It will take some time, but I am sure any man can be taught to be a gentleman. Why, Mister Smith, I can see you now dressed in your finery and attending parties in the grand salons of London."

We laughed together, but I noticed Mister Smith's eyes traveling toward the man standing behind us at the wheel of the ship.

"Beggin' yer pardon, me Lady, but I best be gettin' to me work now. We can practice another day."

"Certainly, Mister Smith," I replied. I refused to allow myself to steal even a glance in Edmund's direction, though I desperately wanted to. I feared if I looked at him, he would know of my wanton dreams and of the feelings I had for him. Feelings I could not deny.

"Seems there be lots o' lessons bein' given aboard this ship of late," Mister Smith murmured under his breath as he scurried away.

Later that day as I sat atop a barrel that rested at the base of a large mast, I gazed out at the sea wondering if there was any truth in the conversation I had overheard between the two pirates that morning. *Could Edmund Drake really find me attractive? Surely that must be the case or why would he kiss me so? But if that were the case, how could I be the cause of the Captain's bad temper?* The memory of our encounter of last night played in my mind, and I sighed as a feeling of warmth washed over me. Deep in my thoughts, I failed to hear Edmund's approach until he rested his warm hand upon my shoulder.

"Milady," he said, "I wonder if I might interest you in some company?"

Perhaps there was some truth to the pirate's theory after all. I faced him, and a shy smile slipped across my lips. "Certainly, Captain."

He took a seat upon the barrel beside mine but seemed to fidget a bit. *So out of character. He portrays the rough and confident pirate, and at other times an elegant gentleman, yet he seems unsure of how to carry himself here with me.* Then I noticed the book in his hand.

"What have you there, Captain?

"Tis a book of sonnets," he said, handing the small tome to me. "I wish to give it to you, Countess, as a gift." I couldn't help but notice how his eyes seemed to grow a lighter shade of green and twinkle with his genuine smile.

Accepting the small leather-bound volume, still warm from his touch, I felt a lump rise in my throat. No man had ever given me a gift before and my heart swelled with joy.

"How sweet of you, Captain," I answered in a voice just above a whisper.

"It would give me great pleasure if you would call me Edmund."

"Edmund, I hardly know what to say." I said, looking up at him.

"Please say you will accept this small gift and allow me to read to you from it."

"Thank you, Edmund. I accept this wonderful gift and would be delighted to listen to you read," I replied, handing the book back to him.

His fingers brushed against mine, and it seemed he allowed his touch to linger there for a long moment as he took the volume from my hand. Our eyes met for the briefest of moments, and I looked away as my heart fluttered.

Opening the book, he began to read. His deep voice took on a tender tone. He spoke softly, privately, only for my ears. The words of the sonnet were those of a man speaking to his lover, and my pulse quickened. Closing my eyes, I imagined being in his arms again, the taste of his kiss fresh in my memory. We sat so close that our shoulders touched, and I did not realize I had come to rest my head upon his shoulder while I listened to the deep timber of his voice softly uttering the sweet words of love. Butterflies fluttered in my stomach at the nearness of him and the scent of his warm skin made me lightheaded. A feeling of total contentment took hold of me, and a deep sigh slipped from my lips.

The sound of his voice combined with that of the sea and wind lulled me into a dream like trance. I could listen to him reciting words of love for the remainder of my days, if only I dared to believe for one moment there was any meaning behind them.

The melody of his strong, deep voice was interrupted by the pulsing sound of running feet rushing toward us. I lifted my head from Edmund's shoulder with a start.

"Captain, Captain, might I have a word?" Smith said breathlessly as he approached. "Beggin' yer pardon, Captain, me Lady." He paused to catch a breath. "Sorry to interrupt, but-"

"Lady Catherine, if you would kindly excuse me," Edmund said and handed the book to me. "Perhaps we shall be able to find a moment to continue this at another time."

He glanced at his Quartermaster and a frown furrowed his brow, but he softened when his gaze came back to me.

Taking the book from him, I said, "Yes, of course. I shall look forward to it."

"As will I." Turning back toward Mister Smith, he murmured, "Smith, this matter best be of grave importance."

"Aye, Captain, it be," the wiry man replied as the two walked away, their voices low in muffled conversation.

I held the book close to my heart. Drunk with the words of love he had read swirling in my head, I leaned back against the mast and closed my eyes.

Chapter 12

Edmund

"Mister Smith, I find we shall have to change course. We have need to make port. Cook tells me the larder is running low," Edmund said as he stood before the great wooden wheel.

"Aye, Captain," the wiry Quartermaster replied.

"I fear we shall be forced to dine on hard cheese and dried bread for supper tonight."

"Nay, Sir. Cook says we be havin' an island meal tonight."

"An island meal?"

"Aye, Captain. The Lady Catherine be makin' our supper. She be claimin' to have fashioned meals o' far less."

"Mister Smith, do you mean to tell me the Countess is down in the galley cooking?"

"Aye."

"Take the wheel. This is a sight I simply must see."

"Captain, beggin' yer pardon, Sir, but her Ladyship, she don't be wantin' no one to be knowin' she ever been in dire circumstances."

"Very well then, I shall wait and see what sumptuous feast awaits us this night."

Lady Catherine

Cook had lent me one of his aprons, which would fit

around me at least twice. I stood in the galley, cleaning and cutting up fish in preparation of our evening meal.

I hope these men like my version of Callaloo. Cooking the meal I often made for my father drew my thoughts to him. I couldn't help but wonder how he had fared. Memories of our island home filled me with such a melancholy sadness and brought to mind songs the island children sang. I smiled as I began to hum one of them. It made the time pass and suddenly I no longer gave a care to the smell of fish.

The meal was ready just in time for dinner. I was anxious for the crew to arrive and sample my creation.

Skepticism was written upon the faces of the men when they entered the galley, yet their hunger won out and soon everyone was seated around the table.

The hearty aroma of the meal arrived moments before Cook appeared with the tureen. Bowls full of the delicious concoction of rice, fish, and beans were laid upon the table. The men were eager to taste what was set before them and were quick to scoop up heaping spoonfuls to sample the fare. I sat in silence, suppressing a smile, awaiting their comments.

"Is this wot become o' them fish we netted today?" one of them asked.

"Aye," the cook replied as he laid out some dark bread.

"What is that delightful aroma?" the Captain asked, entering the galley with a smile.

"Her Ladyship calls it *Callaloo*, and it be right tasty," the cook answered.

Edmund's eyes met mine. With one eyebrow raised and a crooked half smile he asked, "Am I to believe you made this meal, Countess?"

"Yes, Captain. I have been known to have made a meal from far less."

"Hmm, well, let us hope it tastes as good as it smells."

"It do, Captain, it sure do," the cook replied.

Edmund took a seat at the table and Cook handed him a bowl full of the stew. He put the first spoonful into his mouth, and I held my breath.

"Countess, what exactly is this?" he asked.

Thinking he didn't care for my cooking, my heart sank to my feet. "It is a dish called *Callaloo* and is quite common in the islands. I would be pleased if you found it to be adequate."

"It is far more than adequate. It's completely delicious."

I felt the sting of a blush at his compliment. "Thank you, Captain."

"No, Milady. Thank you."

That night, after we had dined, Mary and I took a stroll on deck to get some fresh air before retiring for the evening and to the confines of our cabins. It was rare for me to be on deck at this late hour, but the cool night air and the spray of the sea were so refreshing. As we walked, we came upon the crew and I was amused watching these pirates engaging in relaxing activities. Some played cards, others rolled dice in a betting game of chance, and some danced around while others played fiddles, a pipe, and squeezebox. I found myself drawn to the sound of the lively music. Standing among them, I clapped and laughed watching the activity and before long one of the pirates called Willy grabbed my hand and pulled me along with him into the dance. Willy was a strapping man with a ragged beard. He looked to be quite a ruffian, but in truth I found him to be a gentle giant. I hesitated at first, not wanting to draw unwanted attention, but saw that Mary, too, had been swept up by Mister Smith and crossed the deck, feet flying and giggles floating on the air.

Although I didn't know the steps, I found the dance exhilarating and quite enjoyable and grew breathless at being pulled from one set of arms to the other and swirled around to the lively tune until steely arms gripped me in a close embrace. The music stopped. I stared up into sparkling green eyes and my breath caught in my throat.

"May I have the honor of this dance, Milady?"

"It is I who would be honored, Captain," I replied in what was little more than a whisper.

"What's 'e doin' 'ere?" Whispers rose among the crew.

"'e ain't never left 'is post."

"Can bet it's the likes of 'er."

If Edmund heard the grumble rolling among his men, he didn't let on. He gestured toward the pirate they called Fiddler and said, "Carry on." With a shrug, Fiddler lifted the well-worn instrument and Jake picked up his squeezebox and together they started playing a tune with a slower pace.

Edmund held me so close I could barely breathe, or perhaps I could barely breathe because he held me so close. His body was strong and warm and the scent of his skin made my head spin. He moved slowly to the music, leading me across the deck with masterful ease. It became a struggle to hear the strains of the waltz over the sound of my heart thundering in my ears when he nuzzled my hair.

"You smell delightful, Milady," he said as he placed a soft kiss upon my temple.

My legs felt like jelly, and I was thankful he held me so tightly lest I fall.

"Captain, you have been aboard this ship for far too long if you find the scent of me delightful, yet you flatter me."

"I find much about you to be delightful, Milady."

"You do not find me to be scrawny and too thin?"

"No. You are quite beautiful. What makes you think you are too thin?"

"My father always told me I was scrawny and that

because of it, he would never make a suitable match for me."

"And you believe him?"

"Yes, Captain, I do."

"Well, let me assure you, you are one of the loveliest women I have ever met, and I believe I have asked you to call me Edmund."

"Yes. That you did. Then it is only fitting, Edmund, that you call me Catherine."

"Yes, Milady."

"You waltz divinely for a man of the sea."

"Now it is you who flatters me, Lady Catherine."

He swirled me around with such zest that he lifted me off my feet and held my body pressed tightly against his. His gaze turned dark and smoldering and he stood motionless upon the deck, holding me to him. I clung to his broad shoulders, my heart hammering against his chest. Caught in the spell that seemed to swirl around us, he lowered his head. Just when I thought he was about to kiss me, the music came to an end and drew us from our trance.

Slowly he released me until I felt my feet upon the deck, then taking my hand he brought it to his lips. Placing a soft kiss upon my fingers, he said, "Thank you for the dance, Milady, it was truly a pleasure." He turned away and quickly walked into the shadows.

He left me standing there among his crew with my legs shaking. I was breathless from the closeness of him and from his kiss upon my temple and my fingers. Warmth spread through me, and I felt lightheaded from the feelings this pirate stirred in me.

The music started up again, but this time not the slow strains of a waltz, but rather much livelier sounds. Standing on trembling legs in the center of the crowd, I watched as men swirled around me, passing Mary among them from arm to arm. Everyone wrapped up in the music once again.

My thought lingered with the man whose waltz took my breath away.

That night as I readied myself for bed, I thought of being in Edmund's arms, and a warm feeling rushed through me. I couldn't help but grin. But when I approached the bed and saw a note and small box upon my pillow, the grin turned to a brilliant smile.

My name was scrawled across the folded paper in his masculine handwriting. I held the note close to my thundering heart for a moment. Butterflies danced in my stomach with the anticipation of what his message would say. I took a deep breath and unfolded the parchment.

Milady,

Thank you for the delightful dinner and an even more delightful dance. It is my fervent wish and deepest desire that you accept this gift as a small token of my gratitude. It would give me great pleasure to see it upon your wrist when next we meet.

Edmund

Heart skittering in anticipation, I opened the box to find a lovely silver bracelet. Threads of delicate silver were woven together into a band and there, hanging from the lovely and delicate threads of silver, was a brilliant red gem carved into the perfect shape of a heart and surrounded in silver to secure it.

Hurriedly I donned the delicate bracelet and fingered the heart-shaped stone. *Dare I hope I stir the same feelings in him as he does in me?*

Chapter 13

Lady Catherine

The next morning I was eager to get up on deck to see Edmund. I donned my light blue gown as Mary said no man could resist me in it because it matched my eyes. Excitement jumped in my stomach as I rushed up the passageway and out into the sunshine to find the Captain, but he was not there. After talking to Mister Smith, I learned that during the night we had dropped anchor close to an uncharted island and that Edmund and a few of the men had taken a launch and gone to explore.

A profound sense of sadness flooded me, and I dragged myself to the galley to get something to eat. Sitting there among the crew, I was told more of the Captain's plan. Should the island prove to be uninhabited and of no danger, a day ashore would be our reward. Delight jumped in my stomach, and I thought my heart would burst with glee. I could not say how long I had been aboard ship, but the thought of going ashore made me giddy.

The sweet aroma of rich soil, lush greenery and wild tropical flowers drifted toward me as the launch neared the beach. It was nearly noon by the time all the small boats had reached the shore. When the craft I was in approached the island, Edmund waded out into the water and lifted me into his arms.

"Fear not, Milady, I shall see you safely and dryly to shore."

A giggle bubbled out of me, and I buried my face against his chest. When we reached the shore, he allowed my body to slide down the front of his and he held me there for the briefest of moments. My heart fluttered as I looked up into his clear green eyes, which danced with amusement. Others moved around us, yet they melted from my sight.

To my amazement, he knelt before me. "Allow me to help you remove your shoes, Milady." *He's so strong, yet with me he's so gentle.*

It was then I noticed he was barefooted and his dark trousers were rolled up to the knee. His warm fingers lingered upon my ankles as he removed my slippers and then tossed them upon the beach. The sand beneath my feet reminded me of my island home and a feeling of joy filled my heart.

Standing, he took my hand in his and said, "Come, Catherine, there is something I wish to show you."

Holding onto his hand, I allowed him to lead me up the beach to where some trees and shrubs provided a small area of privacy. Leading me into the shade, he reached under a bush and produced a colorful bouquet of exotic island flowers he had tied with a dark ribbon.

"Oh, Edmund, they are beautiful." The fragrance of the wild blooms smelled sweeter than any perfume.

"Not nearly as beautiful as you, Milady," he said, drawing me into his embrace.

The sounds of activity we had left behind us seemed to vanish. I looked up into his deep green eyes and he held me close to him. "I wish to memorize everything about you, Catherine."

"Why, when you see me daily?"

He remained silent, and when I rested my head against his heart, he sighed deeply.

"Edmund, there is something I wish to tell you."

"What is it?" He drew away from me and gazed deeply into my eyes. Concern etched upon his brow.

"As you know when you took me from the ship that day, I was bound for London to be married to the Duke of Devonshire."

Something flashed behind his eyes for a brief moment but was quickly gone. "Yes, I am aware of that."

"But what you may not be aware of is that my father arranged the marriage, and it is one I was not anxious to enter into. Having never met his Grace, I was given to understand that he is an elderly gentleman."

"Yes, I believe the Duke of Devonshire is quite on in years."

"What I want to tell you is . . . well . . . I prayed something would happen to prevent me from ever reaching England and from being forced into a loveless marriage to an elderly man I had never met."

He chuckled, and fearing his rebuke I rushed on.

"However, I did not wish for pirates. I had seen pirates once when they came to our island."

"I am deeply wounded to find I am not the first pirate you have encountered."

"Yes, actually you are. I managed to escape those who attacked our island."

"How did you accomplish that?"

"I took the children from the orphanage and we hid in the empty tomb behind the parish church, so we were unharmed. The outcome was not so pleasant for some."

"That was a very brave thing to do, Catherine. I feel it safe to say I do not know any other woman who possesses your courage."

"Thank you, Captain, but you must realize that when I prayed for something to happen to prevent me from reaching England, I never asked to be captured by fearsome pirates. Do you think less of me?"

He laughed. "Think less of you, no."

"What amuses you then?"

"I have been called many things in my life, Milady, but never an answer to someone's prayers."

He placed a soft kiss upon my forehead. "Come, we should get back to the landing sight. This is an island of plenty, and we are to lunch here on the beach."

A great smile spread across my face.

"This pleases you, Milady?"

"Yes, very much."

"I thought it might. Come, I have a few more surprises in store for you."

Holding my hand, he drew me beside him and we walked hand-in-hand back toward the others.

The pirates had outdone themselves. Wild game birds roasted over open fires, and I nearly drooled when the aroma drifted to me. Vast plates of fruits and wild vegetables were laid out, and Cook drew roasted potatoes from the fire. Deep red wine accompanied our meal, and we took our fill of it all.

"I do not believe I have ever eaten so much food or taken so much wine." I leaned against Edmund as we padded barefoot along the beach. The sounds of fiddle music and the laughter of the group we left behind drifted to us across the sand.

"Do you miss your home on the Island, Catherine?"

"No, not really, but I do miss the children."

His eyebrow rose. "Children?"

I couldn't help but giggle. "Oh, not my children, the island children." He looked relieved.

"I taught them to speak English and to read. As I mentioned, there is an orphanage on the island and I visited it frequently. The children there loved to hear me read. They have nothing, yet it takes so little to make them smile. I wish I could have done more to help them. Reading to them was a small thing, but it made them so happy."

"You love children, don't you?"

"Yes. I hope to have some of my own one day." A frown creased my brow at the thought of my uncertain future.

"I have known many women of privileged birth and none of them speak so passionately and lovingly about children. In fact, for the most part, they view them as an inconvenience and simply ignore them."

I laughed. "I believe you have found I'm not like most women."

"Aye, you will garner no argument from me on that point."

"And what of you, Captain Drake? Do you dream of settling down one day and having a brood of children?"

"Aye, I hope to settle down one day, but I don't know about having a brood of children. I would be happy with a few."

"Do you have any brothers or sisters?" he asked.

"No, my mother died of consumption when I was a child. What of you? Do you have any siblings, perhaps a brother who is also a pirate?"

His expression grew dark for a moment. "No, no one."

I sensed a change in his mood so I did not query him further. We walked hand-in-hand in silence along the beach for a few moments, enjoying the sound of the surf and the feeling of the sand upon our feet.

"Are you happy, Catherine?"

"More than I have ever been."

"I have something I wish to give you. Another surprise," he said, drawing me along toward some large rocks at the water's edge. Lifting me into his arms, he carried me through the shallow pool of water where the tide lapped against the stones. Being held in his strong arms gave me a feeling of security I never experienced before. A warm sensation filled my heart and I rested my head against his shoulder. He held me closely as he waded through the water. The sound of the thundering waves was surpassed by the thundering of my heart. He sat me upon one of the large rocks and climbed up beside me.

"Why is it you do not fear me? It puzzles me that you never did."

"I did on the first day, but I would never let you see that. From the moment you came into my life, you protected me and made me feel safe, despite the fact that you are a fearsome pirate. You are courageous and unlike any man I have ever known, but still, there must be something that you fear, Captain."

"Aye, I fear not being able to save those that I love."

He grew pensive so I did not press him for details and I couldn't help but feel he was not accustomed to sharing his feelings and especially not his fears. *Unable to save those he loves.* I wondered who it was he had loved and lost and why this strong man felt responsible for not being able to save them.

Questions burned on my lips and when I was about to voice them, the waves crashed against the rocks with a great thundering sound and sent sea spray high up into the air. I jumped in surprise.

"The sea is a powerful mistress," he said.

"One I would imagine it would be difficult to pull away from."

He did not reply, but after a moment he asked, "Are you ready for your next surprise, Milady?"

"Yes." I couldn't keep the giggle of excitement from my voice.

"Close your eyes then and do not open them until I tell you to," he instructed. "Now put out your hand."

I did as he asked and was rewarded with the feeling of something rough, cold, and wet resting in the palm of my hand.

I must have frowned because a chuckle came from deep in his chest.

"What is it?"

"Open your eyes and see."

There in the palm of my hand sat an odd-shaped shell that had been pried opened.

"What is it?" I asked again.

"That, my dear, is an oyster."

"An oyster?"

"Yes, some believe them to be a culinary delight and quite the aphrodisiac, but if you look there you will see its hidden treasure."

I peered closely to find a beautiful pearl.

"Oh my! Is that a pearl?"

"Yes."

"Why Edmund, it's beautiful."

"It is, and it's yours."

"Oh, Edmund." I wrapped my arms around his neck and hugged him to me.

"We shall have it placed in a mounting and perhaps string it on your bracelet with the ruby heart."

"Thank you, Edmund. You dote upon me fiercely."

"Captain . . . might I have a word?" Smith called from the shore.

"That man certainly could do to work on his timing." Edmund scowled.

"It's all right. We probably should rejoin the others."

He hopped off the rocks into the shallow pool and again lifted me into his arms, cradling me there like a child. For a long moment, we stared into each other's eyes.

"This day has been for you, Catherine," he whispered.

Warmth filled my heart and something unfamiliar . . . feelings I could not name, feelings for this handsome pirate captain. "Thank you, Edmund. It has been the most pleasant day I have known."

He waded back to shore and gently set my feet upon the sand.

"I will hurry along and find Mary," I said, not quite sure of how to excuse myself gracefully and afford the men a measure of privacy.

"Me Lady," Smith greeted with a nod of his head.

I smiled my acknowledgment to him, but as I retreated to allow them a moment, I was surprised when I overheard Smith admonishing Edmund. I didn't want to listen, but I couldn't help myself and slowed my pace.

"Need I remind ye o' the prize . . . and that prize ain't The Countess," Mister Smith said.

"Smith, you forget your place."

"Beggin' yer pardon, Captain, n' with all due respect, aside from the ransom, need I remind ye o' the mission?"

"No, Mister Smith, you need not remind me of my duties," Edmund growled at his Quartermaster.

"Ye fancy the Countess, that be plain to see, but Captain, ye must cast aside yer desires, not only for the good o' the mission, but for the good o' the Countess as well."

I heard Edmund's frustrated breath. "You are right, of course, Mister Smith. I shall endeavor to keep my distance from her."

Icy fear washed over me, as if someone had doused me with a bucket of cold water. The prize? Was that all I meant to him, a means to a ransom? I felt foolish, and more than that ashamed for allowing myself to be lulled into believing he had any feelings for me. With tears stinging my eyes, I picked up my skirts and scurried toward the group sitting around the fire.

Chapter 14

After that I rarely saw Edmund and when I did, his demeanor was cool and guarded, his gaze dark and foreboding. A constant knot had settled in my stomach and I lost all signs of my appetite. No longer wishing to spend time on deck, I took to spending all my time in my cabin. One day as I sat reading, a timid knock sounded upon the door.

"Enter," I called out, expecting it to be Mary. But much to my surprise Tobias Smith appeared, hat in hand, fingering the brim nervously.

"Beggin' yer pardon, me Lady, might I come in?"

"Certainly, Mister Smith. Has something happened?"

"Aye, somethin' happened all right, but that's not why I be here."

"What is it then?"

"I came to fetch the maps."

"Oh, yes, the maps." I followed his gaze to the desk, where the drawings lay scattered.

"Aye."

"Take them, take them all. Honestly, I would be happy to be rid of the clutter."

The wiry man scurried about gathering up only those that he needed and quickly made his way back to the door.

"For the life o' me, I don't know who be in a darker mood of late, ye or the Captain," he said under his breath.

"Will that be all, Mister Smith?"

"Nay, Miss."

"Yes, what is it then?"

"Well, me Lady, it be the crew."

"The crew? What is wrong with the crew?"

The quartermaster shifted his slight weight from one foot to the other.

"What is it, Mister Smith?" I snapped.

"They be missin' yer presence."

Despite myself, I felt my heart soar and my lips twitch upward. *Someone on this godforsaken journey actually missed me.*

"We, that would be the crew, and me as well, we be a wonderin' if perhaps ye might find it in yer heart to agree to come and have yer evenin' meal with us?"

Despite my resolve to stay as far away from the black-hearted Edmund Drake as I possibly could, being limited to the confines of a ship, my heart softened at the request of the wiry little man who had grown to be my friend.

"I suppose that could be arranged."

A broad smile lit up his face. "Thank ye, me Lady."

"Please notify Mary of the change in plans if you would be so kind."

"Aye, me Lady, and thank ye."

After that night, everything seemed to be back to normal, except for the way things stood between Edmund and me. He did not take his meals in the galley, and Mister Beckett stood fast at the wheel. Captain Drake remained nowhere to be seen.

One day while walking along the deck arm-in-arm with Mary I broached the subject.

"Mary?"

"Aye, Miss."

"You seem to be spending a good deal of time with

Mister Smith lately."

"Aye, Miss, but if that displeases ye—"

"No. No, not at all." I smiled. "I was just wondering if perhaps you and he ever talked . . . well . . . about the Captain."

I couldn't bring myself to look at her and I cast my gaze toward the deck.

"Aye, Miss. Sometimes. Truth be known, Tobias is at his wits end, he is."

"Why so?"

Leaning her head closer to mine, she whispered, "The Captain has been sharin' quarters with Tobias and frankly, Miss, Captain Drake has been in a right foul mood of late. Tobias has taken to sleepin' in a hammock strung up here on the deck."

"Has Tobias mentioned anything to you about getting us off the ship? Have they had any word that the Duke would pay the ransom?"

"I ain't broached the subject with Tobias."

"Has he mentioned anything to you about a mission?"

"Mission? Nay, Miss, not a word."

When we reached the prow of the ship and turned to make our way back to our cabin, I was surprised to see Captain Drake at the wheel. Butterflies danced in my stomach and my heart leapt to my throat when his eyes met mine and lingered there. But when he dragged his gaze away from mine and looked out to the sea, my heart sank into a sea of disappointment and it must have been written all over my face, for my timid maid placed her hand upon my arm and said, "I'm so sorry, Miss."

"Sorry? Whatever for?" I managed to say in a hoarse whisper, trying to hold back the stinging tears threatening to spill from my eyes.

"I know ye fancy each other."

"Don't be silly, Mary. I mean nothing more to him than means to a ransom."

Later that day, I asked Smith to bring water for a bath. The tension in my neck had developed into a nagging headache, and I longed to relax in the warm water. Mary found my bath salts, poured some into the tub, and the fragrance of jasmine swirled through the cabin.

"Thank you, Mary, you may leave. I wish to be alone to relax, and I believe I can manage a bath on my own."

"Are ye certain ye won't be needin' me, Miss?"

"Yes, I'm certain. You could use some time to yourself as well, I'm sure."

"Thank ye, Miss."

After she left the room, I shed the heavy gown and stepped into the tub. The scented water swirled around me, its heat seeping into me and the tension and headache slowly slipped away. As my body relaxed, my mind relaxed as well. Not having slept well for days was taking its toll and the warmth of the relaxing bath quickly lulled me to sleep and I felt my head tip back and rest upon the rim of the tub.

Again Edmund haunted my dreams with his hooded green eyes. Heat spread through me as his full lips caressed mine and his warm hands cupped my face.

"Umm, Edmund," I whispered.

"You are truly lovely, Catherine."

The heat of a yearning I had never known before rushed over me and throbbed in the center of my womanhood, even in the dream.

"The mere sight of you renders me helpless. Although I have tried, I can stay away from you no longer," he said and lowered his lips again to mine.

My lips parted slightly to allow his tongue to explore the depths of my mouth. Half lifting myself from the water,

I wound my damp arms around his neck and pulled away the ribbon holding his hair back. *This dream feels so real*, I thought as he gently cupped my breast. His kiss burned with urgency and his breathing grew quick and raspy. I moaned with desire as he gently rolled his fingers over my taunt nipple.

"Catherine, my love. I want you," he whispered as he drew me to him, lifting my wet, naked body from the water.

"Never stop kissing me, Edmund," I murmured, eager for the dream to continue. But nothing happened. He was not kissing me, but holding me close to him, cradling me as if I were a child, naked in his arms, while bath water ran off me soaking his clothes. Confusion swirled in my sleep-numbed mind.

As my senses drew me from my dream, I was filled with sadness at the thought of being pulled from his arms, but even in my semi-awake state, the warmth of his embrace still surrounded me. My eyes slowly fluttered open to look up into Edmund's deep green eyes as he lowered his lips to capture mine.

Chapter 15

At first his kiss was gentle. His warm lips took mine in what seemed like a sweet embrace. He drew my bottom lip into his mouth and I gasped. My response pleased him and he deepened his kiss. His breath was ragged and he held me even closer. His tongue ran along the outline of my lips. My mouth opened and the tip of my tongue touched his, inviting, exciting. I wanted him to invade me, all of me. His body was warm and strong and his chest muscles tightened as I twisted in his arms and pressed my naked chest against him. The material of his wet shirt rubbed against my hard nipples. I wanted to feel his naked chest against mine. My breathing grew quick and ragged and his breathing matched mine. I was frantic with a need to touch his muscular chest. He drew his lips away from mine as a light rap sounded and the door opened.

"Ye best be gettin' out o' that water, Miss, afore ye . . . Oh my!" Mary's cheerful voice dropped to silence.

Edmund's eyes bore into mine. For the first time in my life, I realized the danger he'd been trying to suppress behind his hooded gaze was that of deep desire, as I now felt it, too.

"Mary, thank heaven you are here," I managed to say, in a breathless voice barely above a whisper.

"Thank heaven, indeed." The maid's voice took on a scolding tone.

"Yes, I-I fell ill, and strangely, by a-a lucky accident, the Captain happened i-in and rescued me from d-drowning in my bath," I finished quickly as heat scalded my cheeks.

I cleared my throat. "Mary, please hurry and bring me a drying cloth."

Edmund shifted me until my bare feet touched the floor, then Mary rushed to cover my nakedness.

He ran a wet hand through his hair, hanging loosely about his shoulders, and bent to retrieve the ribbon from the floor.

"Thank you, Captain, for rescuing me," I said, holding myself with as much dignity as anyone standing wet and nearly naked could muster.

"It was truly my pleasure, Countess. Now if you would kindly excuse me, I must change out of these wet clothes," he answered, then, turning on his heel, retreated without another word.

As soon as the door closed behind him, Mary faced me. "Wot the devil be goin' on here between ye and the Captain?" she demanded, her arms folded across her chest.

"Whatever do you mean? There is nothing going on." The words sounded false, even to my ears.

"Don't ye be lyin' to me, Miss. The Captain fancies ye, that be plain to see, but to find ye in his arms wearin' nothin' but yer altogether."

"Mary, as I told you, the Captain happened in just as I grew faint. He merely rescued me from drowning in my bath."

"And I suppose he was revivin' ye back to life with his kiss."

"Mary, you forget your place."

"Nay, Miss. My place is to watch out for ye and protect yer virtue from cads such as the Captain. How do ye expect to present yerself as an untouched maiden to the Duke of Devonshire if ye allow that scoundrel of a Captain to steal yer virtue?"

My stomach turned at the thought of the old duke's intimate attention. *How could I bring myself to tolerate the touch of anyone other than Edmund?* I swallowed the lump of emotion that swelled in my throat.

"You're right of course. I shall endeavor to keep my guard up against the Captain's advances." *Could I? Did I even want to?*

"Aye, as shall I. Now, we best be gettin' ye dressed. It nearly be time for our evenin' meal."

After she helped me into a fresh gown and brushed my wet hair, she said, "I shall be movin' me things in here promptly, Miss."

"What? Why?" The thought of never having another private moment with Edmund drained every ounce of joy from me.

"Aye, I can't permit that cad another chance to 'ave at ye."

"That's not necessary, Mary."

"Aye, Miss, it be necessary, and from what I witnessed here today, well overdue."

Arguing with her was pointless and would accomplish nothing but to further her resolve.

"Very well then. Please advise Mister Smith that we shall take our evening meal here, in the privacy of our cabin."

Mary scurried across the deck to find Tobias Smith standing at the wheel while Captain Drake paced behind him, a dark scowl upon the Captain's handsome face. She feared his stern rebuke as she approached, but was determined to have a word with Tobias. Much to her surprise, Captain Drake graced her with a smile.

"Beggin' yer pardon, Captain."

"Good afternoon, Mary. What is it? Is something amiss?"

"Aye, Captain, might I have a private word with Mister Smith?"

"Is the Countess still feeling ill?"

"Nay, she be fine thank ye. I just be needin' to speak with Mister Smith."

"Certainly." He glanced over to his Quartermaster. "I'll take the wheel, Smith."

The wiry pirate turned the wheel over to his Captain and took a few steps away with the maid for a private word.

"Wot be the problem?" he barked, yanking his cap off his scruff of white hair.

"Don't ye be barkin' at me, Tobias Smith."

"Forgive me, me dear. The Captain be vexed and ridin' me nerves."

"Wot is amiss?"

"Nothin's amiss. He said he's in need to make port is all." Smith shifted his weight from one foot to the other, casting his glance everywhere but to Mary's face.

"Make port? As in visit an island?"

"Aye."

"Did we not just spend a day upon an island?"

"Aye." He fingered his cap.

"Do he have a hideout then in some secluded place?"

"Aye, but it ain't seclusion he be wantin'." The wiry sailor danced nervously when Mary raised an eyebrow in question.

"The Captain, he be in need o' some female companionship, if ye gets me meanin'."

"Indeed! The scoundrel." *Rather he cool his lusts with some trollop than with Lady Catherine.*

"Wot brings ye in search o' me?"

"Oh, I nearly forgot meself. The Countess wishes me to inform ye we'll be takin' our evenin' meal in the privacy of her cabin."

The corners of his mouth dropped upon hearing the news. "I be truly sorry, Tobias, but I cannot leave her side.

After . . ." She clamped a hand over her mouth, afraid she'd betray Catherine.

Tobias nodded, quickly catching what she'd left unsaid. "Aye, perhaps that be the cause of 'is dark mood and 'is pushin' to make port."

"Perhaps."

She scurried away. Tobias returned to his place at the wheel.

"So, Mister Smith, Mary Chadwick thinks me a scoundrel?" Edmund raised a brow at his quartermaster.

"Aye. Ye heard then?"

"Aye, I heard."

"Captain, ye gots ears wot can 'ear a mouse fart, if ye don't mind me sayin'. Still, ye be best served if ye keeps yerself clear o' the Countess."

Chapter 16

The following day *The Lady Victoria* drew close to an island, but the Captain dropped anchor outside of the bay leading into port. Knowing we would be going ashore, I dressed in my most comfortable pale green gown and matching slippers. I knew with the lack of the ocean breeze, I would find the heat to be fierce while walking about on the island. When I came up on deck, the smells of spices, rich soil, leather, and the pungent odor of horse dung mixed with the brine of the sea as the scents traveled on the wind and carried toward the ship. Rushing along the deck to catch up with the Quartermaster, I called out, "Mister Smith?"

"Aye, Countess," he answered, hardly slowing his pace.

"Why have we stopped here? I thought the Captain was anxious to make port," I said breathlessly, running alongside the wiry pirate.

"Aye, Countess, that he is, but with ye aboard, we can't pull into port. It be far too dangerous, that, so we be droppin' anchor 'ere and rowin' a launch in."

"I see. Well, Mary and I shall make ready to depart at your notice."

"Nay, Miss, ye not be goin' ashore."

"I beg your pardon?"

"Ye not be goin' ashore," he repeated.

"And why not, pray tell?"

"It be a rowdy place, that, full a trouble . . . pirates, some who'll not give a thought to 'avin' his way with ye and slittin' yer throat after."

"But it is my wish to go ashore."

"Sorry, Countess. Captain's orders." Smith began his familiar dance from one foot to the other as he cast a sideways glance.

"To devil with the Captain and his orders."

"Me Lady, I must insist."

I realized too late that his sideways glance served as a warning.

"Is there a problem here, Mister Smith?" Captain Drake asked.

"Nay, Captain."

"Yes, Captain, there most certainly is a problem," I contradicted.

"Countess?" He raised an eyebrow.

I longed to slap that smirk from his face.

Mustering what I considered to be my most authoritative and condescending tone, I replied, "I wish to go ashore."

"Unfortunately, that is not possible."

"Why not?"

"It is far too dangerous. You and your maid shall remain here aboard *The Lady Victoria* together with a few of the crew, who have ever so graciously volunteered to remain aboard as your guards."

"Guards? Surely you cannot believe I have any intention of trying to escape."

"It is not an escape that worries me, but rather an abduction." He started to walk away.

"Captain," I called after him.

"Countess?" he said, facing me once more.

"Are you telling me that you fear someone will abscond with your kidnapped prisoners?"

"Yes."

"And of course your men will be far too engaged in drinking and whoring to guard me so that I might be afforded the joy of a day ashore."

"Precisely."

"Captain, I demand to be allowed to go ashore."

"Countess, why must I continually remind you that you are, in fact, my prisoner, and as such, you are in no position to be making demands? Now, if you would kindly excuse me, my crew awaits."

He left without another word or even a backward glance and climbed into the launch, which was lowered down to the water. I watched the men row away from the ship and toward the island, and anger burned deep in my gut.

"You shall be sorry, Captain. I know not how, but I swear it . . . you will regret the day you denied me and left me behind," I said aloud, slamming my fist on the rail.

"Ah, Miss, there ye be," Mary called breathlessly as she rushed to my side. "Have we missed the launch?" She busied herself tying her purse closed and adjusting her skirts.

"Yes," I snapped.

"When be the next one then? I be anxious to get ashore." She adjusted her unadorned bonnet.

"There will be no next one. Captain Drake has forbidden us to go ashore."

"Forbid us? But why?"

"He fears his kidnapped prisoners may be kidnapped."

"Countess?" a young male voice interrupted.

"Yes, what is it?" I sighed, turning to find the cabin boy, Jake, who, since our climbing adventure, had been assigned to kitchen duty. Just the thought of my part in his demotion filled me with such guilt I couldn't raise my eyes to meet his.

"Countess, the Captain he say to keeps me eye on ye and for me to keeps ye out of sight."

"You mean to tell me not only am I not allowed to go ashore, but now I am to be confined to my cabin?"

"Aye."

"Very well." Turning to Mary, I said, "Since there is no threat, I shall retire to my cabin. I wish to have some time to myself, and I am sure you could find something to keep you occupied as well."

In behavior befitting my station, I held myself tall and made my way down to my cabin. The only outward indication of my ire was my slamming the cabin door behind me.

Rage burned in me and I flung the books and maps from Edmund's desk. And as his maps scattered to the floor, I stomped on them. Rushing to the table, I took up the knife that lay on the forgotten tray of food and frantically stabbed the surface of the table until, panting for breath, I burst into tears.

Day faded into night and still no launch returned. Boredom won out, and I decided to go to bed, but tossed and turned as sleep eluded me. It was not yet dawn when I heard a shout from above, "Make ready, a launch approaches."

Finally. Breathing a sigh of relief, I rolled over to face the wall.

That was when the first pistol shot rang out and running footsteps echoed above me. The hair on my neck stood on end and I shot out of bed, recalling the day of my abduction from *The Tempest* as I pulled on a robe. In the dim predawn light, I stumbled toward the door. *Mary, I must find Mary,* I thought as I yanked the door opened and made my way to her cabin.

She and I huddled together in the middle of her cabin. The sound of approaching heavy foot falls echoed off the walls.

"Oh, Miss, 'ere we go again. I pray we are not ill treated," she whimpered.

Goose flesh rose on my arms as the door to the tiny cabin slowly opened.

"In here, there be women," yelled a man dressed in black from head to toe.

Hoots and hollers came from the passage, and I held onto Mary as tightly as I could.

Rough hands pulled me and dragged me up to the main deck. Still my grip of Mary's hand held firm. My gaze wandered over the deck. My breath quickened and heart thundered when I saw the lifeless bodies of those who had chosen to remain here as my guardians sprawled dead upon the deck. Tears stung my eyes as my glance fell upon Jake, who could not have been more than thirteen, lying in a pool of blood.

Rough hands pulled me away from Mary and tossed me into the launch.

"Mary," I screamed.

"No, no. Ye can't take her. Take me instead," she screamed at the pirates.

Turning toward the maid, one of the pirates growled, "We be leavin' ye 'ere to tell yer Captain Drake that Blackbeard said if he tries to pursue us, the girl dies."

The darkly clad men jumped into the launch and lowered the small boat to the sea.

Shaking uncontrollably, I sat huddled, hugging my knees as the black-clad men rowed the launch away from *The Lady Victoria* and into the fog that danced across the dark surface of the sea.

Finally, a man's voice echoed over the water. "A launch approaches. Who goes there? Be ye friend or foe?"

"We be crew, Jacobs, ye idiot. Now lower the ropes."

Before long, the launch was being hauled to the deck of a large ship that stood shrouded in the fog and predawn darkness.

Meaty hands grabbed me and passed me to someone who tossed me to the deck. Scrambling to my feet and gathering my courage, I was quick to find my voice.

"I demand to see your Captain."

Their laughter filled the air.

"She got spirit, that she do," one man said.

"Aye, that she do, but we best bring her to the Captain lest our heads roll."

As they pushed me along before them, I chanced a look around. The ship was dark, as if it had been painted black and the men aboard were also dressed in black.

Someone shoved me from behind and I stumbled down the steps leading below deck. The dampness of the fog clung to me and pulling my nightclothes tighter around me, I made my way along the narrow passage with as much dignity as I could muster. My limbs shook visibly and I felt the flood of warm tears streamed down my cheeks.

One of the men shoved me aside and, stepping before me, knocked on the door at the end of the passageway.

"Enter." The single word was uttered by a deep, rough voice, and a shiver ran down my spine at the sinister tone it held.

The pirate pushed the door opened and pulled me by my hair into the well-lit room.

A scream burst from me at the sight of the fearsome pirate who sat behind the large desk. He chuckled. "Please, Miss, have a seat."

Still pulling me by the hair, my captor shoved me into the high-backed wooden chair before the great desk.

"She be quite a beauty, ain't she, Captain?"

The dark Captain's stare at his crewman could have frozen the devil himself. The pirate grew quiet and the Captain's gaze shifted back to me.

"Welcome aboard *The Queen Ann's Revenge*," the fearsome pirate captain said, but his voice held little welcome.

Like his crew, he was dressed completely in black. His long black hair and beard surrounded his rugged and deeply lined face, giving him a fierce and dangerous look.

"I am Edward Teach, Captain of this fine vessel. Perhaps you have heard tell of me?"

"No, I cannot say that I have," I answered. My voice trembled and sounded strained and tight, as if someone other than me had answered.

"Forgive me, my dear, perhaps you would recognize another name that some have called me. Is the name Blackbeard known to you?"

I couldn't suppress my gasp, and as it escaped me, I brought my hands up to cover my mouth.

He laughed. "I see that you find that name to be familiar. Now that you know who I am, would you kindly tell me who you might be?" he asked.

My throat closed and my mouth went dry, but I refused to give into the fear that threatened to render me helpless. I swallowed hard. "Lady Catherine Nettleton, Countess of Dorset," I choked out.

"Countess, is it? Well, the information our spies provided has proved to be correct. I understand you, my dear, are worth a pirate's ransom." The humor in his voice was not reflected in his deep-set eyes.

I clasped my shaking hands together and placed them in my lap. Stiffening my spine, I replied sternly, "So it would seem."

"We shall see." He shifted the stare of his steel blue eyes to the rough pirate standing beside me.

"Make sail to Ocracoke Island, Mr. Newsome. That will be all," he ordered.

When we were alone, he said, "I understand the Duke of Devonshire was quite distraught when he received word of your capture. Perhaps he shall be willing to negotiate a handsome price for your return."

"Only if I am unharmed, and my virtue remains intact."

"You are a naïve girl, but you do have spirit." He laughed.

I gifted him with my most vicious glare, which only served to further fuel his humor.

"You are quite beautiful, Countess."

"Do you plan to ravish me then?" My lip quivered despite my attempt at firm resolve.

"Ravish you? As appealing as that thought is, the answer is no, but I do have plans for you."

"Plans?" The hair rose on my arms and up the back of my neck.

"Aye, Countess. I plan to school you in the art of pleasuring a man."

Chapter 17

Edmund

Sitting in the corner of the darkened tavern with my back to the wall, I sipped my ale and watched the members of my crew enjoying the bounty of women eager to spread their legs for some coin. Some of the women were even pretty, yet none held any interest for me. I couldn't help but wonder how I could have ever been eager to be here.

"What be amiss, Captain?" Smith asked. He set his tankard of ale down upon the table and flopped down into the seat beside me.

"What gives you the idea something is amiss?"

"Ye be wearin' a scowl as black as night upon yer face. I was o' the mind ye had a hankerin' for some female company, yet ye be sittin' here gettin' into yer cups on yer own."

"I was just thinking of Lady Catherine. Have you ever noticed how her blue eyes sparkle like the sea when she laughs?"

"Aye."

"She haunts me, Tobias. I have had countless women in my time, but none have captivated me as she has. Have you ever known such a woman?"

"Nay, Captain, can't say as I 'ave."

"Despite the fact that she is our prisoner, she has taken to the crew. She reads to them, finds humor in their jokes, and dances with them. Hell, she even forced them to bathe."

"I was the one-"

"Come now, Mister Smith. You can't fool me into believing that."

"Well, give a bloke some credit for tryin'."

"She was abducted by our crew and she has shown nothing but bravery in the face of adversity. I must admit, I have known men who show less courage."

"Aye. As have I."

"What I mean to say is it's not merely a lustful desire I have for her, I admire her."

"Aye, she be quite somethin'." He sipped his ale and we sat together in silence for a moment. I had revealed too much of my feelings to the Quartermaster, and the looseness of my tongue was probably due to too much ale. I resolved not to elaborate further.

"Well, Mister Smith . . . you need not sit here with me. Go and find yourself some companionship."

"Be ye certain, Captain?"

"Yes, go. No need for both of us to spend our time sitting alone with our ale."

"Aye, Captain, thank ye, Sir."

Smith drained his tankard and ambled toward a table of ladies who seemed eager to earn a night's wage.

I sat there falling deeper into my cups, haunted by blue eyes, pouty pink lips, and the memory of her lying wet and naked in my arms. In as much as I was in such a hurry to get here, I now could hardly wait to return to my ship, to Catherine. *With the score of women I had been with, how is it I can think of nothing else but bedding that slip of a girl?*

But it was more than that. The memory of her laugh and how easily she found humor with the crew caused something to twist in my gut. Thoughts of her reading to them, the curve of her neck, the smell of her skin, the way she returned my kisses. *Where did she ever learn to kiss like that? She has bewitched me and befuddled my mind. No other woman had ever affected me so. Get a grip, man. Look around you. There are many here to choose from whom could certainly ease the lust burning in your blood.* My eyes roamed the room and landed on Roxanne. The buxom blonde had always made sure she was available to me whenever we made port here. She was seated at a table and surrounded by men, whom I am certain were vying for her favor. When our eyes met, a seductive smile spread across her full and painted lips. Rising from her seat, she sauntered toward me.

"Evenin', Captain."

"Good evening, Roxanne."

"It's been a while since I laid me eyes on yer 'andsome face."

"Aye. That it has."

"Ye be lookin' for some female company to ease your troubles?"

My gaze ran over her, standing there beside the table dressed in a faded red gown that revealed nearly her entire bosom. Normally I would have been quite interested in a romp with the experienced tart, but as I drained my ale, thoughts of Catherine flooded back to me, and I found Roxanne to be paling in comparison and totally unappealing. *Perhaps having another ale would help.* I flagged down the barkeep, and the tentacles of uneasiness wound around my gut.

"Perhaps some other time, Roxanne," I answered and flipped a coin her way.

Her eyes darted toward the coin on the table and she smiled her sweetest smile in an attempt to be coy.

"Be ye certain, Captain? Ye know I gots the cure for wot ails ye." She leaned over, exposing her breasts.

"Yes, I'm certain. My deepest apologies, madam."

"Don't ye be tellin' me, ye be taken to liken the boys?"

I chuckled. "No, madam, I'm simply not in the mood."

"I ain't never known ye to not be in the mood. 'Sides that, ye know all too well I can do things wot'll gets ye in the mood."

She leaned closer and, placing her hand upon my manhood, began to massage me through my trousers.

The thought of being intimate with her turned my stomach and taking hold of her hand, I lifted it away from me.

"Roxanne, I'm not in the mood."

She held herself tall, and her spine stiffened.

"It be your loss, Captain," she said and after snatching up the coin, made her way back to her table of admirers.

Leaning my head back against the wall, I closed my eyes, but for the longest time sleep eluded me.

Finally succumbing to exhaustion, my eyes closed and I found sleep.

Catherine stood upon the deck of The Lady Victoria, *but she looked fearful. Suddenly dark arms snatched her away and dragged her down to the dark water. "Help me, Edmund," she screamed. I tried to grab her, but I was too late. Too late to save her. She was gone, dragged away beneath the darkness. A large pool of blood stained the deck of* The Lady Victoria *and a trail of blood floated upon the dark waves. "Edmund, help me."*

"Catherine," I whispered. I sat up with a start, and found myself still leaning back against the wall in the dark corner of a nearly empty tavern. My breathing was rapid and I was in a cold sweat. With many more hours until dawn, I sat back and tried to find some rest. But sleep was impossible as I could not shake the feeling of dread that curdled in my stomach.

After spending a troubled and sleepless night in the tavern that smelled of stale ale and sex, I met the men at the launch as planned. Some were dreadfully hung over but all appeared happy for having had the time to see to their needs.

Not having been able to shake that uneasy feeling, I was eager to get back aboard the ship and put my back into rowing alongside the men. But as the launch drew closer to *The Lady*, my apprehension grew. No one came to the rail to announce our arrival and lower ropes to raise the launch to the deck. Instead, lifeless ropes hung from the rails, unattended, and the ship bobbed in the tide in an eerie silence. Fear prickled up my spine, and I said a silent prayer that nothing had happened to Catherine.

"Captain," Smith whispered, "somethin' be amiss here."

Unable to control the feeling of dread that overpowered me, I leapt from the launch into the sea and swam the remaining distance to the ship. Grabbing hold of one of the ropes that lapped in the water against the side of *The Lady*, I climbed up and over the rail.

Mary sat on the deck sobbing and covered in blood, Jake's head in her lap. My eyes scanned the blood-stained deck, but they appeared to be alone.

Rushing to her side, I knelt, and in as calm a voice as I could muster, I asked, "Mary? What has happened here?"

"Oh, Captain, it were awful," she answered with a blank stare gazing off into the distance.

A groan escaped Jake's lips, and I was thankful he was still alive.

"Mary, where is the crew?"

"I not be sure, Captain, but I think the evil vermin dragged their bodies to the brig and locked 'em away."

"Mary, were they killed?"

"I cannot say," she whispered.

"Captain, what 'as happened? Do ye mind helpin' us draw up the launch?" Smith yelled from below. Ignoring him, I grabbed Mary by the shoulders, now with both hands and probably a bit more roughly than I intended, I shook her. "Mary, Mary, look at me."

Turning her blood and tear-streaked face to meet mine, her eyes held a vacant stare.

"Where is Lady Catherine?"

"They took her, they did."

My heart thundered in my chest. "Who, Mary? Who took her? Who did this?"

"The men wot was dressed all in black . . ."

My heart nearly froze in my chest at her words.

"What men? How many were there?"

"They said they was leavin' me to warn ye not to follow lest they kill her." She sobbed hysterically now.

I grew frantic with the idea that this could be the work of my sworn enemy.

"Please, Mary. Did they utter a name? Do you have any idea who may have done this?"

With a look of madness and quivering lips, she whispered a single name that made my blood run cold.

"Blackbeard."

Chapter 18

Edmund

"This is my fault, Smith," I said as I paced back and forth behind the quartermaster, who stood before the great wheel.

"How could ye have known this were to happen?"

"Despite trying to keep a distance from her, I should never have left her side. If anything were to happen to her, I shall never be able to forgive myself."

"Don't berate yerself, Captain. We'll get her back. Do ye have a plan?"

"Aye, to find Blackbeard, reach down his murderous throat, and rip his black heart out. I swear to you, Smith, if he touches her, if he does anything to harm her, compromises her in any way, I'll kill him with my bare hands."

"If anyone can find him, Captain, it be you. We been closin' in on his trail for nearly a month now. Ye could have captured him any time if ye had a mind to."

"Aye, I had a mind to, but my orders were to drive him toward his favorite hideout on Ocracoke Island, and not to capture him unaided."

"Aye, but ye never took into account he might snatch the Countess."

I shot my darkest glare at the wiry little man holding steadfast to the wheel. I fiercely felt the need to choke something and struggled to rein in my anger. After all, this was entirely my fault. My fists balled at my sides.

"Captain, I know ye fancy the girl."

Laughter erupted from deep in my chest, which brought a look of confusion to Mister Smith's face.

"I have not gone mad, nor am I laughing at you. I'm laughing because I wish it were only that I merely fancied the Countess, but you see, I find that I'm in love with her."

Finally admitting this to myself, and actually saying the words aloud, flooded me with a deep sense of relief.

"Well now . . . it be about time ye admits it."

My confusion must have been written upon my face.

"We all seen it, plain as the day is long, but now, Captain, wot be yer plan to retrieve her?"

"We sail to Ocracoke Island."

"An' wot will ye do when ye find her? Wot of the Duke? Wot of yer ransom demands?"

"The devil with the ransom. I no longer care about any of that. Catherine is all I care about now."

"Wot o' the girl, then? Ye must do wot's best for Lady Catherine, and that may not be a life as the wife of a sea going bloke. But better the wife of a Duke, living in a fine house, having the life of a Duchess."

His words hit me hard like a punch in the jaw. Damn him.

"You're right, Mister Smith. I love her and want what is best for her regardless of how I feel, yet I can hardly allow myself to even think of having to give her up."

The Quartermaster remained silent for a long moment, then he asked, "Wot will ye be willin' to give for her safe return?"

"Anything, Smith, my life if need be. I was unable to save the only other woman I ever really loved, and I will not lose this one. Failure is unacceptable."

Smith's eyebrow rose. "Ye once loved another?"

"Aye, Smith. My mother."

"Ye would give yer life even if it means ye be givin' her over to the Duke to be his wife?"

"Aye."

"Aye, just as I expected. Then we best set our course to Ocracoke Island."

Chapter 19

Lady Catherine

It seemed like forever until we finally approached the sprawling house that sat at the end of the channel. The house was bigger than the one we lived in on the island and had a wide porch with white pillars. Well hidden by trees that had Spanish moss hanging from them, it seemed to be the perfect hideout. Blackbeard walked toward the wraparound porch, pulling me up the steps and toward the door.

"Countess, welcome to my humble abode," Captain Teach said as he ushered me into the enormous foyer of the grand house.

My head snapped up at the staccato sound of a woman's footsteps rushing toward us, but a grin spread across the Captain's lips, somewhat softening the fearsomeness of his appearance. It was obvious he knew who approached.

One of the most beautiful, voluptuous women I had ever seen rushed into the room. Her dark hair was swept up, held in place by combs adorned with sparkling jewels. Her gown was the shade of robust red wine and made from a material that seemed to float around her like a cloud. Her lush lips were painted the same shade as her gown, and her darkly lined chocolate brown eyes danced with excitement as she hurried to greet the pirate.

"Edwardo, at'a last you arrive." Her husky voice held a sensual quality, and her Italian accent was musical.

"Contessa, how lovely to see you once again," he said, lifting her hand to his lips.

Her gaze fell to me. She wrinkled her nose, as if she smelled some rancid stench, then she snatched her hand away from the pirate.

"Who is this?" she demanded.

"This is Lady Catherine Nettleton, the Countess of Dorset. Countess, this breathtaking vision is the Contessa Theodora de Lorenzo." Her name slipped off his tongue like a song.

"It is a pleasure to make your acquaintance, Contessa," I said.

"Why she dressed in bedclothes?" she asked, narrowing her eyes.

"This is what she was wearing when my men captured her."

"Why you bring her here, *me amore*?" Despite the sweet tone in her voice, her eyes flashed as she glared at the dark pirate.

"My dear Contessa, I wish to make her your student."

"Hmm, you want me to show this shapeless girl how to make a man pant for her?"

"I do."

She walked around me, eyeing me. I felt like an animal at auction and half expected her to check my teeth.

"What say you, Contessa?" the pirate asked.

The fiery Contessa clapped her hands, and a tall black man dressed completely in white with a smooth bald head appeared at the door. The glow of the candlelight gleamed upon his baldness and reflected off his golden hoop earrings.

"*Si*, Contessa." His child-like voice was barely more than a whisper.

"Nameed, please take this girl to the bathing chamber and make her ready for my inspection." Despite her enchanting Italian accent, the word 'inspection' made my stomach tighten.

"As you wish," he said with a bow of his polished head.

"Wait," I nearly shrieked, and everyone's eyes turned to me.

"Yes, Countess?" the pirate lord replied.

Fear gripped me at what the fearsome pirate planned to do. My throat closed and I could hardly speak. "Inspection?" I managed to utter.

"Aye, the Contessa will examine your body and decide how to best accent your, shall we say, assets."

My cheeks burned at the thought of being physically inspected.

"Ha!" the flamboyant Contessa spat. "This stick has no assets."

"Contessa," the dark pirate cooed, "only you could take this sliver of a girl, and transform her into a Courtesan."

"*Si*, Edwardo, this is true."

He smiled at having so easily coaxed her to his will.

Courtesan. I knew not the meaning of that word, never having heard it before now, but I couldn't help the uneasy feeling that crept into my gut.

"Nameed, take her to the bathing chamber and get her out of those rags," she ordered.

"Wait!" I said in what I intended to be a stern voice, but even to me sounded very much like a cat squealing. "I'm not taking my clothes off in front of him."

"Nameed is a eunuch," the Captain said.

"That matters not to me." I held my head high.

The Contessa flew into a rage, and turning on the pirate rattled off at him in Italian. Although I could not understand a word she uttered, I strongly suspected she was not happy. They argued, and finally the Contessa turned to me and said, "You, stick. You come with me." She swept from the room in the rustle of swirling skirts and a cloud of fragrance.

The Contessa occupied several rooms in the grand house, all of which were lavishly appointed and decorated in deep, rich, colors reminding me very much of plates of lush ripe fruits, but my mouth dropped opened when I followed her into her bathing chamber.

An oversized brass tub occupied the center of the room and could accommodate two people with ease, and I wondered why anyone would need such a large tub. But my heart ached with a memory I struggled to suppress when I saw the great tub was completely surrounded by floor-to-ceiling mirrors.

"Close you mouth, stick, and take off those rags you wear." Her words assaulted me as if she had slapped me across the face and my jaw snapped shut.

I did as she asked, for I dared not defy her. She circled around me, surveying every inch of my body, not only directly, but from different angles in the mirrors. I could not raise my gaze from the floor and tears streamed down my heated cheeks.

"What you cry for?" she snapped.

I couldn't find a voice to answer her.

"Men no want to make love, if you cry all the time."

"M-m-make love?" I stammered, still unable meet her gaze.

"*Dio Mio*! What you think a Courtesan do?"

"I-I do not know."

"*Madonna, mio,* help me!" She flung her arms into the air and swept from the room yelling, "Edwardo, *vieni qui,* come here."

I stood alone in the room, confused. I didn't understand. *Had I done something wrong?* When I heard the dark Captain's raspy voice in the adjoining room, I scrambled to cover my nakedness. Their raised voices carried to my ears.

"This stick, she have no shape and she cry all the time. You ask me for a miracle."

"*Si, mi ama*, you can do miracles."

"Edwardo, this is going to cost you."

"Work your magic, *Signora*, and I shall pay anything you ask."

"And what you plan to do with this stick once I turn her into an object of desire?"

"Why, sell her to the highest bidder, of course."

Their laughter echoed off the walls of the bathing chamber and seemed to swirl around me as tears streamed down my cheeks and my heart raced. Feeling both hot and cold at the same time, the waves of nausea won out, and I spewed the contents of my stomach into the oversized tub.

Chapter 20

Lady Catherine

After hours of poking and prodding and a sumptuous dinner I couldn't eat, I was finally shown to my room, the bedchamber adjacent to the rooms occupied by the Contessa. My room was not nearly as luxuriously decorated, but quite comfortable. Donning clean bedclothes provided by the Contessa, I slid between the sheets eager for sleep. I lay there in the dark staring up at the ceiling wondering if the dark-clad pirates would come into my room and ravish me in the night. I was so tense I couldn't sleep. It felt as if hours had passed, but when no one came, my body finally relaxed, and my thoughts turned to my timid maid, Mary. I had never been apart from her for more than a few hours, and she certainly must be frantic with worry. I knew Edmund would have returned by now and would keep her safe.

Tossing and turning, trying to sleep, my thoughts were consumed with memories of green eyes, full of longing, and my heart wrenched.

"Edmund," I whispered softly into the night.

The pain of his absence was like nothing I had ever experienced. A knot gnarled in my stomach and a deep void burned in my chest. I lay awake in the big ornate bed for what seemed like hours. The huge bed had a dark wooden headboard that was carved and inlaid with gold. Tall bedposts reached up to the ceiling and a canopy of white cloth hung over head. Mosquito netting hung from all sides of the canopy just like my bed in my island home, a home I would never see again. *Would I ever see my father or Mary again? And what of Edmund?* Tears fell, soaking my pillow. I finally cried myself into the dreamless sleep of exhaustion. My last thoughts were of green eyes.

The following morning, I was relieved to find Captain Teach had departed and left me in the capable hands of the exuberant Contessa. We sat out on the veranda overlooking the inlet, me in my nightclothes, which were all I had, and the Contessa in her pink silk robe that was adorned with ostrich feathers.

I stared out at the narrow waterway that snaked between the overgrown trees whose branches tickled its surface. No one would imagine such a grand and sprawling home could be hidden in this swampy area. Despite the warm sunlight, a shiver came over me as I stared at the sun's rays dancing upon the calm water.

"Why you no eat? No wonder you a stick. *Mangia!*" She glared at me across the breakfast table.

"I'm sorry. I don't know what could be wrong with me, but I'm not hungry."

"*Madonna, mio,* I kill him if he bring me someone who is'a sick. What's a matter? Where it hurts you?"

"I am not ill." I drew myself up tall and clenched my jaw.

She stared at me for a long time and then put her attention to her breakfast.

"Today we gunna find you some proper clothes." The Contessa's voice drew me from my thoughts.

I sighed, but remained silent.

"I never see any woman who no like new clothes. If that no make you happy, I don't know what will."

I gazed at the sparkling blue water. *You are a fool, Catherine, if you think he would ever come after you. You meant nothing to him, nothing more than a pirate's ransom and a woman he thought to pass his idle time with.* Another deep sigh escaped me.

"Come, let's see what I find that we could make to fit you."

I rose from the table and followed her in silence.

"You may be a stick, but you not so bad. We make you look like a princess, wait, you see."

"Where are you taking me?"

"To look in my trunks of clothes, we find something for you, you see."

I walked along beside her. "Contessa, why are you here?"

"Edwardo captured our ship. He took me and kept me here as his prisoner. I decided better to be his mistress than his prisoner. He provides me with beautiful clothes and more gems than a princess. It's not so bad."

"Has he mistreated you?"

"No. Not yet."

"I have heard he had a wife he allowed his men to bed."

"I no see any woman here." The Contessa gazed around the room, her hands following her gaze in a grand gesture.

"I have heard she mysteriously disappeared. Are you not fearful of what will happen when he tires of you?"

"As long as I keep him entertained, he keep me. I no think about what happen when he change his mind."

"Has he forced you to er . . . entertain his men?"

"No. In all the time I was here, you the only person he bring to the house."

"Don't you miss your homeland?"

"*Si*. Better for me no to think about that."

"Aren't you afraid he will one day kill you?"

"At first I was afraid, but not now."

"Don't you think about trying to escape?"

"No. I think if I try to escape, then he would kill me. So I no think about escape. One day the chance for that will come, and that will be the day I think about it. But today, we think about finding some clothes for you, eh?"

Days of endless instruction of intimate encounters passed. The Contessa showed me how to carry myself with confidence. Despite the way we were thrown together, I was growing fond of her.

"Hold you head up, cast you gaze low," she would say. "Move you hips when'a you walk" or "Smile, but only you lips—no show'a you teeth." One day during a very serious moment while watching myself in a hand mirror as I practiced what she called my "bedroom smile" I stuck my tongue out at her. We laughed together. It no longer fazed me that she called me "her little stick" and being here wasn't all that bad as long as the pirates were gone and I was with the Contessa. She seemed almost like a mother to me, a mother I never had and no matter what happened, she would always have a part of my heart.

She had several gowns, which she altered to fit me. Most of them accented my ample bosom and tiny waist. I had always thought myself to be too thin, but in these dresses that were properly sized to my shape, I felt beautiful, for the first time in my life.

After what seemed like an eternity, finally Captain Teach returned. I wondered if he had any word of Edmund. I rushed along behind the Contessa to the grand foyer to greet the dark pirate.

"Edwardo, at'a last," the Contessa said. Her crisp skirts rustled as she swept into his embrace. After giving her the attention she demanded, he turned to me, yet addressed the Contessa.

"You have created a miracle, Contessa. She looks ravishing."

"I tell you she look good, but she know nothing."

"I have every confidence that you are capable of teaching her all she needs to know."

"Edwardo, something wrong with that girl," she said in lower tones.

"Wrong? What is wrong with her? She looks fine to me."

"What'a you know? She sad all the time. She cry. She no eat. If I didn't know better, I would say she in love."

"In love?" He laughed a full and hearty laugh.

"*Si*. You took her from her man, and now she full of grief for him."

Love. The word echoed in my mind and even stronger in my heart. *Could it be possible? Had I fallen in love with Edmund Drake? What a fool I am!* Anger burned like hot coals in my gut. *How could I have allowed myself to be so stupid as to fall in love with a man who only saw me as a means to a ransom?* My hands balled into fists at my side as I tried to rein in my ferocious need to punch something.

I stood in the Contessa's bedroom with my hands on my hips. "You want me to do what?" I shrieked.

"I want you to watch," the Contessa said with a sensuous smile. She half sat, half lay upon a purple velvet chaise in the corner of her room. I paced before her.

"No, I could never even dream of doing such a thing. There must be another way."

"I can only tell you so much. The rest I must show to you."

"I couldn't." As I faced her, heat flushed my cheeks.

"Look at you."

"What? What is wrong with the way I look? I dressed myself in accordance with your exact specifications."

"Not the clothes. The cheeks, the cheeks. You blush at the mention of anything, of everything."

"That is exactly my point. I would never be able to be present in the same room watching a couple doing . . ." I felt the heat stinging my cheeks intensify and could not even bring myself to say the words.

"No one even know you there. You watch from behind the curtain." She rose from the chaise and walked over to the deep wine-colored velvet drape that hung from the ceiling in the corner of her chamber. She ran her hand along the velvet as if admiring the rich feel of the fabric. Then turning to me, she continued, "Tonight when I entertain Edwardo, you sit here behind the curtain and you watch." She drew back the drape to reveal a white brocade chaise draped with a white fur of some kind, a tiny table adorned with candles and silver goblets, and a plush brocade chair.

Fire burned from my neck to my hairline.

"*Madonna mio*! How you ever going to learn if you no can watch? And stop with the red face. What man ever going to want to be with a woman what's always ashamed?"

That night I helped the Contessa as she instructed me in how to transform her bedroom into a salon of sensual desires.

"It's not all only about the sex. You got to make the man hungry. He no gunna eat if he no hungry. *Si*?"

She swept about the room, placing a good amount of candles in strategic places. I helped her to move the floor-length mirrors closer to the bed and arrange the wine goblets on a silver tray on the bedside table, but I became confused when she came into the room with an armful of blood red roses.

"Sit," she said as she took a seat at the table in the corner of her oversized bedchamber. I did as she requested.

She only smiled as she sat at the table and began to pull the rose petals off their stems.

"Stop! Why are you doing that? You're spoiling them," I cried.

She sighed. "You still know nothing."

After she had stripped all the blossoms off and threw the stems away, she gathered the fragrant and delicate red petals in her skirts and sashayed toward the door.

"Come with me."

Rising from my seat I followed her and was amazed at what she did next. She scattered the petals along the hallway and cast a few of her scant lace undergarments here and there among them, making a lush, blood-red trail leading to her bed. She glided back into the room and then carefully laid the remainder of the delicate red petals atop the white satin bed covering. Proceeding to the grand chest, which stood at the other end of the room, she selected a garment made of sheer black lace.

"You see? Now when Edwardo come, he find me wearing this, waiting for him in the bed of roses. You think that make him hungry?"

I swallowed the lump in my throat, realizing I would be watching this entire scene unfold from my hiding place behind the curtain.

"Will Captain Teach know I am watching from behind the drape?"

"You no worry. Edwardo no be thinking of you."

Later that night I sat in the richly upholstered chair behind the curtain watching the Contessa. I was afraid that if Captain Teach found out I was there, it would mean my end. I was scared of being caught, but even more nervous about watching him in an intimate act with the Contessa. But she was putting on a grand play, and I was her audience. As I observed her performance, I imagined being held by Edmund as he made love to me. Although I had the general idea of what it was like to make love, seeing the act this close, I found my body reacting in a way I'd only felt with Edmund. I could tell that although the Contessa claimed to be performing, she enjoyed Blackbeard's touch. Her mouth fell open and her head dropped back as the infamous pirate entered her. It felt almost sinful to be studying them, but I found my breathing quicken as I watched them please each other. I longed to do those things with Edmund.

The memory of his kisses and the thought of his touch caused liquid heat to rush to my center. Clenching my jaw, I pounded my fist upon my leg. *Steel your mind and force him out of it. You meant nothing to him. Besides, you will never see him again, so stop pining.*

Chapter 21

The couple had fallen asleep and I felt it was safe to leave so, taking my shoes off, I crept out of the room and back toward mine. The hour was late, but the sound of voices echoed from the entrance. *Who could be here at this hour?* I walked past my room and tip-toed down the hallway toward the sound of the voices.

As I neared the foyer, I realized the conversation was coming from the dining room. My bare feet were chilled from the cold of the floor, but I ignored it as I easing my way down the hall, stopping in the shadows just outside the door.

The voices were that of men, several of them. The sounds of dishes and glasses clinking accompanied by the aroma of food led me to believe they were enjoying a midnight meal. *How many men are in there and who are they? I had better hurry back to my room before-*

"Well, well, well. Wot 'ave we 'ere?" A man's deep voice coming from behind me startled me.

He grabbed me by the arm and dragged me along with him toward the dining room.

"Well gents, our luck 'as taken a good turn. Lookie wot I found." He shoved me ahead of him into the well lit room.

About twenty of Blackbeard's crew, all dressed in black, sat around the dining room table eating, and they seemed just as surprised to see me as I was to see them. My pulse instantly raced and I felt as if my heart would burst from my chest. *I thought the Contessa had said Captain Teach never brought his crew to the house.*

A quick glance around the room confirmed my fear that there was no escape.

The pirate who dragged me in from the hall grabbed my hair and pulled me down into his lap as he sat in a chair at the table.

"Well, girly. When we took ye from Drake we was all just waitin' for our chance to have at ye . . . and it looks like we is finally gunna gets that chance." He pulled me closer to him. Although he didn't reek as badly as Mister Taylor had, he was far more dangerous. Edmund wasn't here to save me from a certain fate. I shook uncontrollably which only made him laugh.

"Don't be thinkin' you is gettin' 'er all to yerself, Newsome. How's about we toss 'er up 'ere on the table an takes turns?" One of the men said.

"Aye," they all said in unison.

Newsome grabbed me by the hair again and rising to his feet, he dragged me along with him. "Okay, but I gets te go first. I don't be wantin' no sloppy seconds."

I couldn't breathe. I wanted to scream, but feared they would slit my throat if I did. My legs felt like jelly when Newsome pressed my back up against the table. Reaching up he grabbed the bodice of my rose colored gown and tore it away. I scrambled to hide my nakedness from the hungry stares of the pirates.

"Jacobs, grab 'er arms," Newsome said, and one of the men jumped up and grabbing me from behind held me tight against his body.

My dress was torn to the waist. The cool night air on my naked breasts caused my nipples to peak.

"Lookie there, she be 'appy ta see me," Newsome said. He reached up and squeezed one of my nipples. I turned my head away from him and closed my eyes. I couldn't bear to watch what I knew would happen next. He lowered his head and sucked my other nipple into his mouth while all the while pinching the other one with all his might. I tried to squirm away, but Jacobs' hold was strong.

"Ye keeps squirmin' again' me like that little Miss an I just might takes ye from behind," Jacobs said.

I cringed when a cheer rose up from the band of pirates who had all risen from their seats and gathered around to watch.

Newsome drew his lips away from my breasts. He pulled a dagger out of his belt and grabbed the waist of my gown. "I wonder wot the rest o' ye tastes like."

"No, please," I begged.

The resounding laughter of the men filled the room. I was never more scared in my life.

He slid the tip of his blade into the waist band of my gown and with one swift jerk, sliced the front of my dress open.

I stood naked before the ogling eyes of these vicious men and shame filled me.

I felt Jacobs' rough hand running up my back side as Newsome's hand slid between my legs.

"How's 'bout you takes 'er from the front at the same time as I takes 'er from the rear?" Jacobs said.

I felt Jacob's naked hardness pressing against my rear end.

"Wait a minute, Jacobs. I wants te taste 'er first." Newsome said and shoving my legs apart, he dropped to his knees before me. "'old 'er steady, Jacobs."

Newsome forced my legs further apart and ran his tongue over my most private place. While Jacobs held my hands behind me with one hand, he reached around and fondled my breasts with the other, all the while rubbing his hardness against my rear.

My heart hammered. I wanted to fight, but knew if I did, I would die. I tried to force my mind to thoughts of

Edmund. I knew then that I would rather die than let these men violate me.

At that moment I lifted my right knee and with all my strength brought it up to Newsome's jaw.

Blood spurted from his mouth as he flew backwards onto his heels. The force of my movement caught Jacobs off guard. My head snapped back and smashed into his face. I felt the warm splash hit my neck and realized it was Jacob's blood. He stumbled backwards, yet he did not fall.

"Ye bitch," Newsome growled spitting blood to the floor. "Ye made me near bite me tongue off. Now yer gunna pay." He pulled the dagger back out from his belt and strode toward me.

I was so afraid I feared I would wet myself.

"Newsome, don't be killin' 'er till after we fuck 'er." Jacobs said. "She split me lip, an I be bleedin' as well, but I be rock 'ard an ain't gunna lets ye knife 'er till I gets off." He slid one hand over my rear and I felt the tip of his hardness as he tried to force it between my cheeks.

Newsome undid his trousers and pulled out his throbbing manhood. He clutched me to him and slid the tip of his shaft between my legs.

I opened my mouth to scream but Newsome put his hand over my mouth.

"Ye scream, ye die," he whispered as he placed the blade of the dagger against my throat.

There was no escape as they had me in an iron hold between them. I closed my eyes as tight as I could as tears streamed down my face.

Just then, a gun shot rang out, the smell of gun powder and smoke filled the air and my attackers jumped away from me.

"What you think you do here?" The Contessa's voice was like a choir of angels to my ears.

The men grumbled under their breath.

"You okay my little'a stick?" She came to my side and putting one arm around me drew me close to her.

I couldn't stop crying.

"I'm gunna take her to her room and when I come back, you better all be gone, if you no wanna die." She said to the pirates as she pointed her gun in their faces.

I don't remember how I got there but the next thing I knew I was sitting in a tub of hot water and the Contessa was washing my hair.

"Did they hurt you, my little'a stick?"

"N-n-no. You got there just on time. One moment longer and they would have brought me to ruin." The tears were flowing and I couldn't stop them.

"You no worry. Edwardo he furious. The men no come here again or they die," she said as she poured warm water from a pitcher to rinse the soap from my hair.

I was numb, but the Contessa understood. Somewhere in the back of my mind I wondered if she had ever been taken by force. She helped me from the tub and after gently drying me and getting me into my night clothes, she helped me into bed.

I felt as if I were moving slowly in a dream. She handed me a glass and told me to drink it.

"What is it?" I asked as I coughed from the strong taste. The sting burned all the way to my stomach.

"Brandy. It help you to sleep now. You no think no more about those men and you go to sleep."

"I'm afraid. What if they come back?"

"You no be afraid. They no come back. I stay right here with you."

I stared at the Contessa, dressed in her pink satin robe with the flowing ostrich feathers. She sat in a chair beside the bed with that gun in her hand and it wasn't long before I drifted off to sleep.

Chapter 22

Edmund

"Mister Smith, the charts indicate we will soon approach the isle of St. Thomas. I suggest we make port," I said. I stood with my hands upon the wheel while Tobias checked the compass and the map.

"But Captain, Sir, I be of the mind ye was in a hurry to get to Ocracoke Island."

"Aye, that I am."

"That blighter Blackbeard already gots a good amount of a head start on us. Be ye sure ye wants to stop n' lets him increase that lead?"

"Mister Smith, you forget that Blackbeard also has a fortress on St. Thomas. We shall go ashore and mingle with the locals. Let us see if we might glean some information as to his whereabouts and the plans of that black-hearted swine. We shan't spend more than a few hours time, and the delay may be worth it to us if we can gain some idea of his intentions."

"Aye, that be a right fine idea, and while we be there, we can stock our larders."

"Good thinking, Smith."

That afternoon, walking with a few men, I ventured into a tavern rumored to be frequented by Blackbeard and his crew. Making my way to the back of the crowded tap-room, I took a seat in the darkest corner. Tobias Smith dropped into the seat beside me.

"Wot can I get for ye?" the barkeep asked. As he ambled toward the table, I noticed he limped upon a wooden peg leg.

"Ale and information," I answered.

"Ale we got, information . . . well, that depends wot ye be wantin' to know and how much coin ye be willin' to part with."

Tossing a coin upon the table, I said, "Buy yourself a drink and come join us, my good man."

The barkeep quickly snatched up the coin and cast me a wary glance.

"Where ye hail from? Sure by your fine speech and your accent, ye ain't be from o'round these parts."

"London, originally, but now the colonies, Virginia to be exact," I offered. "But we will speak more of these things over a drink." I glanced at the empty chair beside me.

Putting the coin in his pocket, he ambled away.

"Captain, don't ye be thinking ye might 'ave said a bit too much?" Smith whispered.

"Nay, I wish him to think me dim-witted. You see Mister Beckett standing there at the bar?"

"Aye. How could I miss yer First Mate?"

"His mission is to listen. Mine is to talk."

"I should have known ye had a plan."

"Always, Mister Smith, always."

The afternoon went exactly as expected. When we returned to *The Lady,* our larders were full and Mister Beckett had some valuable information. The barkeep openly complained to him of my idiocy and bragged of how he'd duped me out of my coin and managed to give me no information of importance. He did, however, impart to Mister Beckett the news he so proudly kept from me; that in two days time the notorious Blackbeard himself was planning a grand party in his fortress here on the island, a party where he would introduce his latest acquisition and newest Courtesan, for sale at auction to the highest bidder.

Upon hearing the news, I found I could barely breathe. My chest constricted and I found it difficult to force the air through my windpipe into my lungs. My heart pounded so loudly I thought surely Mr. Beckett could hear my body's protest to the news. It had to be Catherine. I needed to get into that party and make sure I placed the highest bid. Since the party was to be held in two days, we had a bit of time, so the three of us sat up into the night devising our plan.

When I finally made my way to my cabin, I sat at the desk reviewing the maps and running the plan over in my mind. It was useless for me to try to sleep, yet I would try, as I did each night. And each night turned into the same torture for me as I lay awake tossing and turning until sleep finally took me, only to then be tormented there by visions of Catherine's crystal blue eyes smiling up into mine, of her luscious pink lips, her smile, of her lying naked in my tub and in my arms, memories of the abandon in her kisses. Memories that drove me mad with a need I could hardly contain. Even a dousing of cold water each morning could not cool the desire that burned in my blood only for her.

Rather than lay there in sheets soaked with sweat, I decided to get up and further formulate my plan. Surely Blackbeard's crew would recognize *The Lady Victoria* should it be seen in port. For any hope of success, we best move the ship well out of these waters. *How many among my crew would need to remain behind to carry out our plan?* While sitting at the desk in my cabin, I gazed at Catherine's things scattered about the room and as I watched the morning light filter through the window I vowed to myself that this time I would not be too late.

Fearing I would be recognized, it was agreed Beckett and I would switch places. We were nearly the same size, although my shoulders were broader than his so it would be simple to swap clothes. He would dress as a Lord of the Court, and I as one of his servants. We were put ashore, together with Smith, Taylor, and a few others, six of us in all. Uncertainty rattled me and knotted in my gut as we stood together on the dock in this busy port and watched *The Lady Victoria* sail away from the island.

"Beckett, we must hire a coach and secure lodging. You are playing the part of an emissary of the Duke and must act accordingly. Lady Catherine's life is in your hands, and I'm counting on you."

"Aye, Captain. My nerves are rattled enough without your constant reminders of the importance of my part in this."

"Sorry, Beckett, I know you realize how much this means to me, how much *she* means to me."

"Captain, might I suggest ye be sendin' Taylor and a few of the others 'round to the other side of the island to secure other escape routes? This way should the need arise at least we won't be runnin' blind," Smith suggested.

"Excellent idea, Mister Smith. Taylor, take a few men and head around toward the pirate fortress. Keep your mouths shut and your eyes and ears opened and above all, be discreet."

"Aye, Captain. We be meetin' up with ye later at the Inn then?"

"Aye, and gentlemen, remain unseen and keep to the plan. Remember, Lady Catherine's safety comes first."

We had hours until the party, but time seemed to stop as I stood at the window in my room watching the docks. When would *The Queen Ann's Revenge* make port?

Just as day slipped into dusk, the great dark ship sailed into the waters of the sparkling blue bay. I watched eagerly as the men disembarked, yet there was no sign of the black-hearted pirate lord I had chased for so long. But my heart nearly stopped in my chest at the sight of the two beautiful women who were guided from the ship.

One of them seemed older, yet her beauty clung to her like morning dew upon a rose. Her dark hair was swept up into an intricate coiffeur and her dark eyes scanned the area. Her brilliant yellow-colored gown accented her voluptuous figure, and she carried herself with an air of confidence as she led her companion away from the dock.

My eyes rested then upon the beauty that walked beside the lush and flamboyant woman. She was far lovelier than I remembered. Catherine's dark hair was also pulled up into an intricate style and held in place by combs adorned with gems that gleamed in the late day sun. Her gown was a pale blue and fit close to her body, accenting her slim waist and ample bosom. The skirt fell full and seemed to swirl around her like a cloud as she walked in the same confident manner as her companion. Seeming to gain confidence from the stares of the men around her, she smiled at them and nodded in acknowledgment, but when she lifted her head and her eyes fell upon the Inn, I felt like I'd been punched in the gut. It seemed she was looking and smiling directly at me. My heart hammered against my chest. As my hungry gaze swept over her, I was taken with a bolt of desire so strong I couldn't breathe.

I watched as her companion whispered something to her and she laughed, and then turned her attention elsewhere. My heart held a heaviness I had never known. My arms ached to hold her. I yearned to tell her how I felt, to whisper sweet words in her ear as I made love to her. I closed my eyes, and my hand rested upon the coolness of the glass. *She must never know how you feel. You can never tell her. You will ultimately have to let her go, for her own happiness.* I swallowed hard, forcing down the lump of emotion that threatened to choke me.

Chapter 23

The Party
Edmund

Smith and I dressed in the modest clothing of a servant, but Beckett was adorned in my most expensive attire as we made our way to the party. Our coach pulled up to the pirate's castle. The stone turret rose up into the blackness of the night sky, and the hair rose on the back of my neck as I prepared to walk into the lair of my sworn enemy. Struggling with the notion of keeping my eyes toward the floor, I reminded myself a servant must never meet the eyes of his betters. We were stopped at the entrance of the great hall where we were searched for weapons. When it was found he carried none, we were ushered inside. Squashing down my need to survey the fortress, I forced my mind on keeping to the plan.

The great hall of the castle bustled with people, both men and women, all of whom were dressed in exquisite and expensive attire. Musicians played soft strains of a waltz, which could hardly be heard over the buzz of conversation.

Negroes wearing white gloves and matching uniforms carried silver serving trays laden with drinks and delectable nibbles. They moved among the throng of revelers offering refreshments to the guests. Looking around the room, one would have thought we were at a party at one of the grand salons in London. But that thought was quick to leave my mind when Smith came to stand beside me.

"'Leave yer weapons at the door.' Do ye suppose that means the black-hearted buzzard will be here after all?" he whispered.

"That matters not. If we are to get out of here with our lives and Lady Catherine, we must not deviate from the plan."

"Aye, the plan. The quicker this be over, the better. This place gives me the willies," he said, his eyes darting around the crowd.

Beckett moved about the room and although he was dressed in the rich clothing befitting an emissary of the Duke, he seemed as skittish as a mouse in a room full of hungry cats. Standing directly behind him, I leaned closer to whisper in his ear.

"Beckett, calm yourself and stick to the plan. You must not be outbid. I have handed in a sealed bid which hopefully will guarantee our success. But no matter, you must play your part and no matter how high the bidding goes, you must surpass it."

As the time of the presentation and the bidding grew closer, the excitement and anticipation that filled the room was nearly unbearable.

"Beckett, take these papers," I whispered.

"What papers?" he asked as I shoved the folded parchment into his hand.

"I have secured passage for Lady Catherine on *The Lady of The Sea* leaving for London on the morning tide. See that she is on it."

"London? But Captain, I thought-"

"Don't think, just stick to your part of the plan and do as I ask."

"Aye." He tucked the papers into his jacket.

"I apologize for adding to your anxiety, Mister Beckett. In the event you should happen to be outbid, do not fret. Remember, I have submitted a sealed bid, which I hope will entice that greedy, black-hearted bastard. Now, get in there and win the prize."

Chapter 24

The Party
Lady Catherine

I stood in the room high up in the turret of the castle. The sound of a waltz being played echoed up from below, but was nearly drowned out by the sound of the crowd. *How many people were down there waiting to buy me, like a slave?* My stomach churned and it was all I could do to choke down the vomit that rose to my throat.

The beautiful sea-blue gown hung in the wardrobe. I stared at it, knowing the time was nearly upon me and I should get dressed, yet I couldn't move.

"Why you no dressed?" the Contessa said as she floated into the room.

"I was just admiring this lovely gown before putting it on."

"Come, I help you."

"Contessa?"

"*Si?*"

"I'm afraid."

"Why you afraid, my little a'stick?"

"I'm afraid of what my future will bring, of being mistreated, of having to be intimate with a stranger."

"You no worry. The man who bid to get you, he get a princess. If'a he spend that much money, he treat you like a queen."

"I know you have taught me what to expect and what to do, but I don't think I will be able to do it."

"Why no?"

"I couldn't abide the touch of a man I didn't love."

"After a while, you will."

It was all I could do to smile and hold back the tears that threatened to spill. In all the time I had been held captive by Edmund and then by Blackbeard, this was the first time the thought of escape had seriously entered my mind.

She helped me into the gown and made some last minute adjustments to my hair. Then she handed me a large black velvet box.

"Edwardo, he give this to me when he first capture me, but I give it to you now. It my gift and I hope it bring you good luck, like it bring to me."

I lifted the lid to find a necklace of diamonds and sapphires, with matching earrings.

"Oh, Contessa, they are beautiful, but I couldn't-"

"Si. I insist." She picked up the necklace and placed it around my neck. After fastening it securely she stepped back.

"Perfecto. It just what you needed. Put the earrings on."

I did as she asked and stepped back for her appraisal.

Her gaze ran over me from head to toe and a frown creased her flawless brow.

"Why you wear that bracelet? It no go with you gown."

"Please don't ask me to remove it, Contessa. It is precious to me."

"It from him, no?"

"Si." I replied in my imitation of her native tongue.

"Ok then, for now, you keep. Maybe no one notice."

I hugged her then. "Thank you Contessa, for everything. For helping me, for protecting me, and for understanding. You're like the mother I never had."

She drew away from me. "If'a I had a daughter, I hope she be like you."

Tears pooled in her dark brown eyes, but she waved her hand and seemed to whisk them away and with a sniffle she said, "Andiamo. Let's go. Edwardo, he waiting." She took my hand and led me to the top of a grand staircase where Captain Teach stood. The buzz of the crowd was overpowering and the smell of food made my stomach lurch.

"Contessa, this is your greatest accomplishment," he said to the woman standing beside him. "And, Catherine, you look more beautiful than I could have imagined. Tonight you will become the Contessa of the Sea."

The Contessa smiled with pride as I was her greatest achievement.

"And now, ladies, the time is upon us." Captain Teach said. He nodded to a man in dark clothing. I watched as the man slipped down the stairs ahead of us. I felt like I was in a dream, a nightmare. Then taking the Contessa's hand Captain Teach led her away.

I stood there, alone at the top of the stairs, just out of sight of the crowd below. I was so scared. My knees shook, my mouth went dry and I was gasping for breath. At that moment my life flashed before me, and just when I thought I couldn't possibly be any more afraid, the music stopped. A man's voice bellowed from right below me.

"Ladies and Gentlemen, may I have your attention. I would like to welcome you to Teach Castle. I ask you to join with me in giving a warm welcome to our host this evening, Captain Edward Teach, escorting the lovely Contessa Theodora de Lorenzo."

The uproar of applause became deafening and terror gripped my soul.

Chapter 25

The Party
Edmund

The music stopped when a tall gentleman dressed in formal black attire appeared at the top of the staircase, which descended into the grand hall from somewhere higher up in the fortress.

"Ladies and Gentlemen, may I have your attention. I would like to welcome you to Teach Castle. I ask you to join with me in giving a warm welcome to our host this evening, Captain Edward Teach, escorting the lovely Contessa Theodora de Lorenzo."

The uproar of applause became deafening and the energy in the room was tangible, as all eyes anxiously awaited the appearance of the notorious pirate. Clenching my jaw, I gritted my teeth as the dark and dangerous pirate came into view. My hand instinctively rose to the scar on my cheek as I stared at the man who'd given it to me. Dressed all in black, his long black locks and beard gave him a fierce appearance. The hair on my arms rose at the sight of him, and I was thankful for the length of the sleeves of my coat. So close, and yet so far, I thought, my hands balling into fists at my side. *Keep to the plan. Capturing Blackbeard is not part of tonight's plan,* I reminded myself.

The flamboyant woman I had seen earlier rested her gloved hand upon his arm as he escorted her to the landing. She was now dressed in a blood red gown that clung to her ample figure and exposed nearly her entire bosom. Her lush lips were painted to match her gown and rubies and diamonds adorned her neck and ears. She was quite beautiful, yet held no interest for me.

"Thank you for coming and welcome to my humble abode," the dark pirate said in a deep and raspy voice. My heart hammered against my chest and I forced down my desire to destroy him. I had spent a good number of years in pursuit of that black-hearted villain, and now I stood across the room, mere feet away from him, and could do nothing.

"It is my great pleasure to introduce, in her debut appearance, The Contessa Catherina de la Mare. The Countess of the Sea."

This is it. My mouth went dry, and I held my breath. The rustle of her skirts announced Catherine's approach. The translucent material of the sea-blue gown clung to her slim waist and ample bosom, yet the skirt seemed to float and swirl around her legs to give her the appearance of a mermaid dancing upon the ocean.

She wore her dark hair pulled up into an intricate style held in place by combs that sparkled with diamonds and sapphires. Matching gems also graced her neck and ears. At seeing the jewels adorning her slender neck, I remembered the silver bracelet I had given her and my eyes darted to her wrist. The delicate silver twine and ruby heart seemed out of place with the rest of her attire, but my heart skipped a beat at the sight of it.

All thoughts of the dark, notorious Blackbeard left my mind as I gazed at her. I couldn't breathe, and I feared my thundering heart would betray me. My stare found her blue eyes sparkling in the candlelight as a smile graced her lips; the pouty lips I longed to kiss. Droplets of sweat formed on my brow and I found it difficult to swallow the lump of emotion swelling in my throat.

Reaching out a hand to her, Blackbeard escorted her to the edge of the landing where the three of them stood. A sharp stab of pain hit me in my gut and the hair rose up the back of my neck at the sight of his hand on her. He slowly turned her around to reveal the soft flesh of her naked back as the fragile material of the gown dipped to caress the curve at the crest of her bum. One lone tendril of her dark hair had escaped her elegant coiffeur and now rested on the fair skin of her exposed back. My mouth drop opened. *How is it she thinks herself too thin? She's stunning.*

One of the other servants standing beside me elbowed me sharply in the ribs.

"Take in your fill, lad. The likes o' us ain't never gunna see such a beauty grace our beds," he chided.

"Rest assured, this lovely vision you see before you remains untouched," the dark pirate said as he turned Catherine to face the crowd once again. "But, be ye not fooled. This beautiful maiden has been thoroughly instructed in the arts of pleasure by the infamous Courtesan, Contessa Theodora de Lorenzo.

"It should be made known to you that I have received a few sealed bids prior to this presentation, but there is only one I wish to entertain. I will speak to Mister Beckett, emissary of the Duke of Devonshire, at the end of the night. Now, let the bidding begin."

A look of surprise crossed Catherine's face at the mention of Beckett and the Duke of Devonshire, yet she hid her expression quickly with a coy smile.

The bidding called to mind the memory of sharks in a feeding frenzy. The flush of color to Catherine's cheeks caused the sting of desire to stir in my blood.

Smith waited beside Beckett as the bidding began, and I took my stand at the back of the room. Despite the distance, I couldn't tear my eyes away from Catherine, who was being scrutinized by the frenzied mob. Her eyes swept the crowd and finally rested upon Smith and Beckett. A quick flicker of recognition flashed in her eyes and the hint of a smile tugged at the corner of her lips, but she recovered quickly. Tearing her gaze away from them, her eyes swept the crowd. *Dare I hope she is looking for me?*

Stop. She can never be yours. For her sake, you must see to it she becomes the Duchess of Devonshire.

Beckett proved to be ruthless in his bidding, and by the end of the night had won the prize. As Lady Catherine was escorted to his side, her eyes finally found mine and for a moment I couldn't move. My desire for her was far beyond physical, but my body responded to the sight of her. I felt as if my manhood would burst from my trousers as I watched the tip of her tongue moisten her lips. Her eyes sparkled as her gaze held mine. My heart thundered, and I wondered if she was experiencing the same rush of desire when her gloved hand came to rest over her heart. Her lips then parted slightly and I couldn't draw the strength to look away. I was nearly panting with need, not only a need to possess her physically, but to possess every part of her, to possess her heart as she possessed mine. I had to force myself to rip my gaze from hers. Emptiness filled my chest where my heart had once been, but knowing she was now safe and her future insured, I turned away and silently slipped out of the room.

Chapter 26

Lady Catherine

Immediately after the bidding, I was whisked out of the pirate fortress and shoved into a waiting coach. Mister Beckett sat by my side and Tobias Smith road with the driver, but what had become of Edmund?

"Mister Beckett, thank you for saving me from what would surely have been a horrible fate."

"You are quite welcome, Lady Catherine, but your gratitude is misplaced. It is Captain Drake who came up with the plan and the coin."

"Please, give him my thanks." My back stiffened against the seat and my heart ached. I remained silent for the remainder of the carriage ride. *Since they were acting as emissaries of the Duke of Devonshire, Edmund must surely have received his ransom.*

When the carriage pulled up to the docks, I was surprised not to find *The Lady Victoria*. Mister Beckett handed me down from the carriage and my feet barely touched the ground as I was quickly ushered onto the large and sturdy ship at the dock.

A lump formed in my throat when I then spied Mary, hurrying across the deck to greet me. Nearly knocking me off my feet, my once timid maid threw her arms around me and drew me to her heart in a strong welcoming hug.

"Oh, Miss, I was a'feared I never would be seein' ye again."

I hugged her close to me, overcome with a feeling of the deep warmth of family as tears ran down my cheeks. "Mary, oh, Mary. I'm so happy to see you."

We cried together for a moment, then, remembering myself, I stood tall and dried my eyes.

"This is as far as I shall be going, Milady, but Mister Smith will be making the entire voyage with you to insure your safety," Mister Beckett announced.

"I truly am grateful to you and to Captain Drake," I said.

"I will be sure to express your appreciation to the Captain. God speed, Milady." And with a stern nod and the glimmer of an unshed tear in his eye, he turned and walked down the gangplank disappearing into the dark of night.

I was delighted to find my trunks had been delivered to the ship, but when I discovered this vessel was bound for London, my stomach lurched. Anger simmered in me at the notion that Edmund must have indeed received his ransom and was now shipping me off to the Duke. *That was his plan all along, wasn't it? He probably was happy to be finally rid of me.*

The trip was uneventful, yet I chose to spend most of it in my cabin. Whenever I ventured out to the deck, the crew leered at me like a starving dog eyes a bone, and I felt unsafe. Even on a ship of pirates I never felt so threatened. I remembered the day Edmund rescued me from the clutches of that scruffy Mister Taylor. A shiver ran down my spine at the thought of it, but I realized I always felt safe around Edmund. He wasn't here to guard me now though, and pain seared my heart as I realized that was of his own choice.

There was a deep emptiness in the center of my being, which had become a physical ache. I could hardly bring myself to eat, but when I gazed at my reflection and saw the loose fit of my gown and the dark circles beneath my eyes,

I managed to force down a few bites. Sleep eluded me and when I finally managed to find it, I found Edmund waiting for me there in my dreams.

Time dragged by, days passed, then weeks, and then the ship finally reached London. The port was teaming with excitement. Everyone seemed in a hurry and it appeared they had somewhere they urgently needed to go. The docks were teaming with ships all loading or unloading cargo, passengers or crates. People and carriages crowded the streets and the aroma of roasting meat traveled to the docks on the breeze. Despite all of this, I could not even manage a smile as I stood at the rail watching my trunks being unloaded. Even after my prayer that something would happen to prevent me from being forced into a loveless marriage with the Duke, I had ended up here regardless.

We were met at the dock by a livery that had been sent to fetch us. So, the Duke had been made aware of my arrival, I thought. Sitting with me in the elegant black coach on the way into town, Mary and Tobias chatted excitedly as they watched the buildings slip by. Overcome by profound sadness as I neared my fate, I remained silent and found it difficult to find my breath. The couple seemed not to notice how distraught I had become, and I was glad for it.

As the coach ambled through London, my gaze traveled over the many grand buildings and I realized how much this city had changed in the eight years I had spent on the island with my father. I wondered what had become of my father. It seemed like a lifetime ago that he stood on the deck of that disabled ship, his eyes begging me not to name him. Part of me wished to see him, to make things right between us, yet part of me hoped I would never see him again. The only two men I had ever loved in my life had both thought so little of me. I meant nothing to either of them. Father thought of me as a means to gain access to a Duke's wealth, and to Edmund

I meant nothing more than the means to a ransom. I couldn't stop the tears from rolling down my cheeks.

The coach turned onto a wide tree-lined boulevard boasting many stately homes.

"Oh, Miss, this be Mayfair, the grandest section o' town," Mary said as she patted my hand.

"Aye, only the best for ye, me Lady," Smith said with his crooked grin.

The coach stopped before the biggest and most elegant house on the street. Mister Smith hopped down and helped Mary and me to the ground.

"I hope the staff has made ready for yer arrival," he muttered, pushing open the wrought iron gate and ushering us up the front walk.

As we approached the house, the ornate oak and stained-glass door was drawn opened by a butler. Although his hair had gone white, the man's face did not show the wrinkles of age. He had a distinguished air about him.

"James," Tobias uttered and nodded in greeting to the butler.

"Mister Smith, please do come in," said the tall butler, dressed in formal attire.

"James, this here be Lady Catherine Nettleton, The Countess of Dorset n' her maid, Miss Mary Chadwick."

"Welcome to Hartington House, Lady Catherine, Miss Chadwick."

Entering the foyer, I mustered a small smile toward James and wondered how it came to be that Tobias Smith was so well acquainted with a rich man's stately butler.

Despite the chill of the day, the foyer was warm and the scent of fresh flowers floated in the air. The entire staff, dressed in their dark servant's uniforms, lined up to greet us and was introduced by the butler.

Mary was shown to the maids' quarters, while James gave me a tour of the house. I couldn't help but note the elegant furnishings and masculine décor. The Duke's home could surely use a feminine touch, I thought, but dared not voice my opinion. Finally, James showed me to my room.

When he opened the doors, the size of my quarters astounded me. The walls were painted in a shade of rich thick cream and the coverlet of the large bed was the color of a deep rich coffee filled with cream. Grand chests stood open, revealing beautiful gowns with shoes and hats to match, and I wondered who those things might belong to. The room boasted a lovely seating area before an oversized fireplace and a huge desk took up the final corner of the room. The entire house seemed to have such a masculine feel, yet this room had been created specifically for a woman. The man who had designed this room must have deeply loved the woman he designed it for.

The windows looked down upon a stone terrace and formal garden, which at this time of year graced me with bursts of vibrant autumn color. Running my fingers down the lace curtain, a deep sigh escaped me. Longing for this type of love amounted to pure madness. Being promised to the old Duke, I knew such a life would be merely a dream for me.

"I trust you find your accommodations suitable?" James asked.

"The Duke of Devonshire has a lovely home," I said, now facing the butler.

"Yes, Milady, but I had not realized you had visited his home. It was my belief you were brought here directly upon your arrival."

"Yes, I was. Please forgive me my confusion, James, but isn't this the residence of the Duke of Devonshire?"

"No, Milady, this is the home of his son, the Marquis of Hartington, but the Marquis requests you occupy it until your marriage to his father."

"And where will the Marquis be staying?"

"The Marquis spends very little time here, and in fact is not in residence at present."

"I see. When will I meet the Duke, then?"

"He plans a dinner tomorrow evening."

"Thank you, James." I tried my best to keep my despair out of my voice. "Would you please see to it that my trunks are brought up and that those gowns hanging there are delivered to their owner?"

"Those gowns are for you, Milady."

"For me?"

"Yes."

"The Duke is much too kind."

"They are not from the Duke, but are a welcome gift to you from the Marquis."

Chapter 27

Lady Catherine

"Miss, wot do ye be wantin' to wear to be dinin' with the Duke tonight?" Mary asked, rummaging through the many beautiful gowns hanging in one of the large chests.

"Honestly, I care little. Please, just select one for me," I answered with a sigh and turned my gaze back out the window.

"Wot do ye think o' this one?"

I glanced back at her to see she held a beautiful gown of deep green and a lump rose in my throat as my mind filled with the memory of Edmund's green eyes.

"No, not that one. Please select a different color," I said in a strained voice.

"Oh, but miss, this one be lovely. Why won't ye wear it?"

"Mary, I do not wish to wear the green one tonight or any other night. Now please select another."

She gave me a quizzical look and muttered unintelligibly under her breath, but she hung the beautiful gown back in the cabinet.

Finally deciding upon a cream-colored gown, she made arrangements for me to have a bath.

The lovely bathing chamber adjacent to my room had been designed in shades of rich cream and taupe to match my quarters. The tub sat in the center of the room and a washstand and basin stood to the side. Drying towels were folded and stored in the shelves of the washstand and they too were the shade of a rich coffee with cream. I surveyed the room, but when I caught sight of the full-length mirror standing behind the tub, a lump formed in my throat and tears threatened. I fought with myself. *Do not allow yourself to shed one more tear over the likes of that scoundrel, Edmund Drake. He only sought to make you his mistress, to occupy his time and cool his lusts until he could be rid of you.* Thank heaven I had not succumbed to his charms and allowed him to steal my virtue. At least I was able to walk away with that intact.

I was quick in the bath, eager to be out of that room. *Tomorrow I must ask James to have that mirror removed from my bathing chamber.*

I grew silent as Mary fixed my hair, and I moved in the slowness of a dream-like state while she helped me into the beautiful gown. I stood before the mirror and had to admit, the way the cream-colored fabric draped across the bodice and drew toward my right hip really cinched my waist and accented my figure. Finally satisfied with my appearance, I was ready to go.

The sleek black coach pulled up before the house, and Mister Smith seemed to appear out of nowhere to assist us.

"Might I be so bold as to say ye look lovely tonight, me Lady," he said as he lifted me into the coach.

"Thank you, Tobias," I answered, sounding far more melancholy than I intended.

He smiled when he lifted Mary in next to me.

"You two have a right fine time tonight dinin' with the Duke."

"Won't you be accompanying us, Mister Smith?" I asked.

"Nay, me Lady. The Duke don't be wantin' to see an ol' goat like me. He be lookin' to meet with his beautiful young bride."

"Thank you, Mister Smith."

"You enjoy your dinner, me Lady," he said, and then his gaze fell to Mary, and he added, "an' I be seein' ye later." He winked, causing color to stain her cheeks.

The coach arrived at the Duke's residence, only a few streets over. His large and stately home somehow lacked the elegance and grace of his son's residence. A footman hurried to the coach to assist us, and we were shown to the door, which was opened by a tall butler who, like James, dressed in formal attire.

"Good evening, Lady Catherine, Miss Chadwick. Welcome to Simmons House. Won't you please come in? The Duke is expecting you."

Mary and I made our way into the foyer, where the butler took our wraps. A perky maid in a gray uniform appeared and showed us into the dining room. The dark wood floors gleamed in the candlelight, but it was the portrait hanging above the fireplace that immediately drew my attention. I stepped closer to get a better look at it. The woman in the painting was a natural beauty, with dark hair, high cheekbones, and fair skin. The elegant style and rich color of her hair accentuated her beautiful deep-red gown. Her hands were folded in her lap and she wore a lovely bracelet of silver twine with a ruby red heart hanging from it.

Exactly like the one Edmund had given me, and my hand flew to the bracelet on my wrist. A young boy who completely resembled her stood beside her in the portrait, his hand resting upon the arm of her chair. Both were smiling as if they shared some deep secret. Their smiles lit their faces and their deep green eyes shone with it. My pulse raced at the sight.

"Good evening, Lady Catherine," a voice sounded behind me. A voice so hoarse and thin it sounded as if it had come through years of burial dust.

I turned to see the elderly Duke sitting in a wooden chair with oversized wheels that was pushed into the room by a young man in a dark gray uniform. The Duke wore a white shirt and black jacket with matching satin lapels, but his legs were covered with a navy blue blanket, and not even the tips of his shoes were visible. I curtseyed. "Your Grace, it is a great pleasure to meet you." I swallowed hard and tried to force a smile.

I rose and stepped closer to him, offering him my hand. His touch was cold. He brought my hand to his thin, wrinkled lips and placed a kiss, which felt as dry as bone, against my knuckles. He smelled like liniment and camphor. Although I was very young when my mother took ill and died, the smell took me back to standing beside her deathbed, and the entire encounter turned my stomach.

"Come, my dear, and let us get better acquainted over dinner."

He motioned toward the table. Servants fluttered around like butterflies in a flower garden, ushering me to my seat and making sure all was in order. When the Duke was certain I was comfortable, he motioned for the staff to begin serving.

He's ancient, I thought. *He is so old, I wonder if he has a servant to feed him. How will I ever be able to tolerate marriage to this man?* A servant placed a steaming bowl of soup before me. My stomach rolled. I lost my appetite just watching the Duke's gnarled and shaking hand lifting the silver spoon to his cold, dry lips. I prayed my disappointment in his aged appearance would not be revealed upon my face.

"Your Grace, you have quite a beautiful home."

"Thank you, my dear."

"I couldn't help but admire the lovely portrait hanging over your mantle. Who is the beautiful woman and handsome child in the painting?"

"I married very late in life and that lovely vision was my wife, Lady Victoria. She died many years ago. The child is our son."

Goose bumps rose on my arms when he said the words *Lady Victoria*, and I forced myself to squash down the memories that flooded my mind.

"I'm sorry for your loss. Did they pass from some illness?"

"She died giving birth to our second child, a daughter, who unfortunately, also perished. Our first child is still alive, although until quite recently, he and I have been estranged. I fear for many years he held me a grudge for his mother's death."

Just then the Duke took to an uncontrollable fit of coughing, and I feared death would take him right there at the table. Servants rushed to his side and unable to tolerate watching the scene playing out before me, I forced myself to avert my gaze. *How could I bear being married to this man? He was older than my own father and even older than his father before him.* My gaze shifted to Mary, but she kept her eyes upon her plate and remained silent.

I suffered through the strained conversation during the remainder of dinner, after which we retired to the drawing room. My gaze traveled around the elegantly appointed room, yet upon closer inspection I found the furnishings to be old and outdated. Tea was served and again I watched his shaking hand lift the delicate china cup to his lips. I imagined his bone-dry lips on my body and a shudder ran through me. Suddenly I felt as if I couldn't breathe and it took all the strength I could muster not to rise from my seat and race from the house.

"Tell me, my dear, how was your voyage from the islands?" he asked.

"It seemed I would never arrive, yet it was uneventful."

"Uneventful! I thought you were captured by pirates. I had hoped you would regale me with tales of a great adventure."

Oh, yes, I surely could tell him a tale of great adventure, but dared not. I simply replied, "Yes, that is true, but there was no adventure. I was merely held their prisoner and much to my surprise, treated with respect and kindness."

"I see."

"I am sorry to disappoint you, Your Grace."

"You are far from a disappointment, Countess. You are more beautiful than I imagined."

"Thank you. You are too kind and you flatter me, Your Grace."

"Please, call me Wentworth."

"Yes, Your Grace."

"Tell me of your life on the island, my dear."

I let my mind run free over the memories of growing up in the heat of the Spice Islands and began to describe it to him in great detail. I told him of the lush vegetation and beautiful exotic flowers, I regaled him with stories of the island children and how I taught them to speak English and how I read to the orphans. I amused him with humorous tales of my discovery of different animals that made the island their home. I made a conscious effort never to mention how I worked the vegetable gardens, cooked the meals, and tended to the stables lest he think ill of me. As I spoke, I cast my eyes to the floor. I could hardly bear the sight of him. Finishing my tale, I asked, "Would you like me to tell you next of the pet parrot I had when I lived there?"

My question was met by silence. Fear took me. I imagined the old Duke to have finally succumbed to death, but relief flooded me I raised my gaze to find he had merely fallen asleep in his chair while listening to my stories.

"Mary," I whispered to my maid, "perhaps we should take our leave now and quietly so not to wake him."

"Aye, Miss," she said, and rising to our feet, we tiptoed toward the door.

That night in the privacy of my room in the stately home of the Marquis, I cried myself to sleep. Yet I could find no relief even there. My dreams were haunted, as they were every night, by soft, warm lips and intense green eyes.

Chapter 28

Lady Catherine

The following morning while at breakfast, an invitation to accompany the Duke on an outing in the park later that afternoon had arrived. I imagined myself pushing him along in his wheelchair, more like a nurse rather than a bride. I sighed deeply and shuffled my eggs around on the plate with my fork.

"Don't be sad, Miss," Mary said.

"Mary, your wedding day should be one of the happiest days of your life, yet when I think on mine, I believe I would prefer death."

Mary smiled at me, but sadness filled her eyes.

"When I imagined my wedding day, Mary, I always dreamed I would be marrying a handsome man, strapping and tall. We would be madly in love and he would sweep me up into his arms and carry me away." I sighed. "Childish fantasies, I suppose."

"Try to find some happiness in it, me Lady. Perhaps the Good Lord will bless yer union with a child."

A shiver ran through me at the mere thought of a physical union with the Old Duke. I rose from the table and walked to the window, where I spent most of my time these days, staring aimlessly out at the day.

"Come now, Miss. Let me help ye ready yerself for the outin'."

No amount of help could ready me to spend time with the Duke, but I forced a smile for Mary's sake.

For the outing I decided to wear my blue cloak with the fur trim. It had a matching hat that I was told was all the rage these days. I was more excited for the opportunity to wear my new hat than I was about seeing the Duke.

The dreadful outing I had expected turned out to be a delightful carriage ride rather than a walk. Mary accompanied me, as always. She sat beside me and remained silent throughout the entire ride. The Duke sat across from me in the open carriage and despite the warmth of the autumn sun, a heavy green plaid winter blanket covered his lap. He wore a shirt the color of rich cream and the green of his jacket matched the green in the blanket covering his legs. As before, the tips of his shoes were not visible and the thought occurred to me that perhaps he had some sort of amputation. My tongue felt twice the size and stuck to the roof of my mouth at the thought of having to be intimate with him.

"You are a vision of loveliness in that hat, my dear," he said in a weak voice, barely above a whisper.

"Thank you, Your Grace."

"Wentworth, please, my dear. You are to be my wife, and it would not do for you to go on calling me 'Your Grace.'"

"Yes, Your Grace." I swallowed hard as the question I burned to ask him rose to my lips.

"Your Grace?"

"Yes, my dear?"

"When will we be wed?"

He chuckled. "Anxious, are you? Not nearly as anxious as I, let me assure you."

A blush stung my cheeks, and I cast my gaze to my lap. Surely he must know it would be a marriage in name only.

"How lovely you are when the color rushes to your cheeks." He reached for my hand and it took all my resolve not to pull away.

"My dear, rest assured, I may be a bit older than you

and in a wheel chair, but I am still quite able to perform my husbandly duties."

The heat rushed from my neck to my hairline, and I could not raise my gaze from the sight of his gnarled claw of a hand grasping mine. I swallowed hard to force the bile back down when I imagined him exploring my body.

"Speechless, I see. I think we shall wed after the Yuletide season, perhaps upon the New Year. This will allow us ample opportunity to get better acquainted, allowing you time to prepare and to await the arrival of our family members."

"Family members?" I lifted my gaze from my lap.

"Certainly, my dear. Your father must be present to give away the blushing bride and my son, of course, will come from the colonies to stand up as my groomsman. I have already summoned them."

The thought of seeing my father again gave no ease to the turmoil dancing in my stomach.

I felt the old Duke's touch fingering the ruby heart on my bracelet.

"I have noticed you wore this same bracelet last evening. I couldn't help but notice it, as it resembles one that once belonged to my late wife, Victoria. I understand only two of its kind were ever made. It appears you have found the other."

"It was a gift, Your Grace, and it is very dear to me."

"I understand sentiment is attached to objects given by loved ones thus making the object dear to us, yet I cannot help but wonder if it is the object we find dear, or the person who has gifted it." Light sparkled behind his aged eyes as he looked at me.

Again I cast my gaze to my lap.

"Catherine, my dear, I sense a deep sadness in you. Are you unhappy?"

"No, Your Grace," I replied, my lie barely above a whisper.

"Is there someone who has captured your heart? Is it perhaps the gentleman who has given you his heart to wear here upon your delicate wrist?"

"No, Your Grace, there is no one." Pain seared through my chest, and I fought to suppress the tears that threatened to come.

As the carriage approached one of the many entrances to the park, we came upon a group of boys hawking papers.

"Blackbeard captured," they yelled. "Governor Spotswood and his navy of Privateers to be honored by the Crown."

"Boy," the old Duke called.

"Sir?" The lad ran to the carriage.

"Let me have one of those papers, son," the old man said, and tossed a coin to the newsboy.

"They have been after that pirate for years. Menace to the seas he was. Glad someone finally did him in," the old Duke said, and he tossed the paper upon the seat beside him.

Strange feelings surged in me. Although he was a notorious pirate and fierce to gaze upon, Blackbeard had never hurt me and, in fact, had actually been kind to me. My heart clenched when I wondered what had become of the Contessa without his protection, and I wondered who the band of men were that had finally tracked down Captain Edward Teach.

My eyes darted toward the newspaper article, but the Duke interrupted with a question.

"Would you honor me by having dinner with me again this evening, my dear?"

"Yes, certainly Your Grace, the honor would be mine." I answered mindlessly, my eyes darting eagerly to the article.

"No need to have your maid accompany you, my dear," he said with a twinkle behind his aged eyes.

"I would feel more comfortable having her there, Your Grace, for proprieties' sake."

Virginia Governor, Alexander Sportwood formed a group of men loyal to the crown. They posed as pirates and roamed the seas hunting the blackguard, Blackbeard. Fierce fighting upon capture . . . Blackbeard cornered . . . Robert Maynard . . . Edmund Drake . . . My heart skipped a beat and my breath caught in my throat at the sight of his name in print. *Edmund Drake?*

The old Duke was talking about the gardens we were passing and naming the late autumn blooms, so he did not noticed my distress. My eyes scanned the paper further . . . *on their way to London to receive special commendations for service to the Crown.* My heart fluttered as a glimmer of hope rose within it. Edmund was on his way to London.

Chapter 29

Lady Catherine

News spread like wild fire that the ship carrying the men who had vanquished the notorious Blackbeard had arrived and the heroes were on their way. Butterflies leapt in my stomach and my hands shook, making it difficult to tie the ribbons of my green velvet bonnet. The clothes gifted to me by the Marquis were rich and exquisite. The green velvet cloak and matching bonnet were among them and I was delighted to have an occasion to don such elegant garments.

"Hurry, Mary, or we shall be late," I called.

"What be the 'urry? Tobias ain't even brung the carriage about yet."

"I heard the heroes are to be greeted by an emissary of the King, and that is something I simply must see."

"Aye, I'm sure it be the emissary ye be so anxious to lay yer eyes upon," she muttered under her breath. "Besides that, won't ye be goin' with the Duke to the ball tonight?"

"Yes," I answered, suddenly deflated.

"You won't be foolin' me none, Miss. I know it be *him* ye be longin' to see."

I lowered my gaze, and Mary placed her hand gently upon my arm.

"It's all right, Miss. I know ye love him."

"Is it that obvious, Mary?"

"Aye."

"Does Mister Smith know?"

"Aye."

"Well, let us hope no one else takes notice," I said as I pulled my gloves on.

I stood as close to the platform as I could get. The huge crowd pressed forward, with everyone struggling to get a glimpse of the heroes. The cheer that rose from the crowd was deafening when the royal carriage approached. Footmen dressed in bright red jackets opened the door and assisted the King's emissary as he descended. Every head bowed, and I fell into a deep courtesy when he approached. I had never seen any dignitaries of the Crown before and upon seeing him, I became overtaken with an emotion I did not expect nor could I explain. It took all my strength not to cry, and I cast my eyes to the ground as he walked past. But when I raised my head my breath caught in my throat as I found myself starring into Edmund's deep green eyes. The cheering of the crowd became background noise to the rushing of my blood thundering in my ears. The people standing around me seemed to vanish away. I stumbled as I tried to rise from my courtesy, and his strong hands grabbed me and saw me firmly to my feet. The hint of a smile tugged at the corner of his lips and his eyes darkened with that same look he'd worn the day he held me wet and naked in his arms. "Catherine," he whispered hoarsely.

But before I could even blink, he was pushed along by the mob and pressed to move on.

"Edmund," I whispered after him. The mere utterance of his name burned like his kiss upon my lips.

Pushing my way through the crowd, I rushed blindly back to the carriage, Tobias and Mary following closely upon my heels.

"Wot be wrong, Miss? Where ye be headed?" Mary called to me over the crowd.

"Away from here. Tobias, please take me back to the house."

His eyes shot to Mary, who nodded. "Aye, me Lady. If that be yer wish."

As the carriage pulled away from the celebration, I buried my face in my hands and sobbed. Mary held me in her arms like a mother held her child and allowed me to drain my sorrows.

Later that afternoon, Mary came to my rooms to assist me in getting ready for the formal celebration at Court. When she entered, she found the drapes drawn and me huddled deep under the covers soundly sleeping.

"Miss," she said softly, shaking my shoulder. "Miss, it be time to wake, time to prepare yourself for the ceremony."

"Mary, please send word to the Duke that I am indisposed and shan't accompany him tonight."

"Be ye ailin'?"

"Yes, please tell his Grace that I suffer from a fierce headache and have retired to my bed."

"Heartache be more the like of it," she muttered under her breath, while making her way out of the room.

I rolled over and buried my face into the pillows. I couldn't bear the thought of seeing *him*. *How could I stand there before the aristocrats of London, on the arm of the frail, old Duke, in front of Edmund? What would Edmund think?* "Don't flatter yourself," I said aloud, "the thought of you never enters the mind of that arrogant poppycock." *What you really should do is put on your most beautiful gown, hold your head up high, and go to that celebration. Let that son of a jackal see what he has given up.* Then the words of the Contessa ran through my mind, *You've got to make a man hungry. He's not going to eat, if he's not hungry.*

"Mary," I yelled.

"Aye, Miss," she cried, hurrying back into my room.

"Have you dispatched the messenger to the Duke yet?"

"Nay, Miss, I was about to do just that when ye summoned me."

"I have changed my mind. Please, come in here and help me ready myself and let us select the most attractive and flattering gown in the cabinet, that green one. Tonight, I intend to turn some heads."

Edmund Drake, by the end of this night, you will not be hungry; you will be starving!

Chapter 30

"Miss, calm yer nerves. Ye be sure to wear a path in the carpet with your pacin'. Don't be frettin'. Ye look like a vision."

"Thank you, Mary. Tonight is important."

"Aye, Miss, I know . . . he'll be there, the Captain, I mean."

"Yes, he will. Mary, I want to thank you for not passing judgment."

"Miss, who am I to judge ye? Besides, yer in love with him."

"Oh Mary, he's unlike any man I have ever known. He's brave and strong, yet when he's with me, he's gentle and kind. He protected me and risked his life to rescue me from the clutches of Blackbeard. And although he had many an opportunity, he never took advantage of me or forced himself upon me. He was a gentleman and treated me with respect. Yes, Mary, I do love him."

"Then ye be doin' the right thing."

I smiled. "I hope you're right."

The dark coach with the Duke of Devonshire's crest upon the side pulled up before the house at the exact hour he had indicated. It was all I could do not to rush out the door and scream at the footman to hurry. Forcing myself to sit calmly in the drawing room, I waited until I was summoned by James, who announced that the Duke's valet had arrived.

Rising slowly from my seat, I swept from the drawing room in a tide of deep green silk that swirled around my legs like the tide. The beautiful gown was designed like none I had ever seen. The rich material crossed over my breasts from either side and swept around my body then gathered at the back, just above my bottom. The skirt was not full and only required that I wear only half the amount of petticoats beneath it. The fabric clung to my hips and gave a slim line to my figure. Mary said the maid told her the seamstress who delivered it said it was all the rage in Paris, but I felt sinful, even scandalous wearing it. It was daring and provocative, and simply perfect for the plan I had in mind for Captain Drake.

With Mary's help, I donned my green velvet cloak and allowed the valet to escort me to the waiting coach. After seating me across from the ancient Duke, he hopped up into his seat, and the coach pulled away from the stately home and headed toward the celebration.

"You look ravishing this evening, my dear," the Duke said.

"Thank you, Your Grace. It is my most fervent wish not to be an embarrassment to you."

"You, an embarrassment? Never. That would not be possible. Why, every man there will be envious."

"You flatter me, Your Grace."

"I speak the truth. I have never seen a more stunning beauty in all my days and I know many a younger man would desire to be named as your future husband."

"Thank you, Your Grace."

"Tonight, I shall introduce you to the emissary of the King and some of the Grand Dames of Court, and we shall announce the date we intend to wed."

"Your Grace, although I will be delighted to be introduced to your friends, perhaps we should postpone the announcement of our nuptials."

"Postpone the announcement? But why, my dear?"

"Tonight is not about us, but rather about those brave men who have finally brought a notorious enemy of the Crown to justice."

"How unselfish of you, my dear. You shall truly make a wonderful Duchess."

A stab of guilt shot through me. I was being anything but unselfish. In reality I couldn't bear the thought of Edmund hearing the announcement. Words of denial to my unselfishness sprang to my lips, but I could not bring myself to voice them.

The coach pulled up before the entrance of the great hall. My hands shook as the valet handed me down from my seat, and my stomach tightened as if I were about to be sick. Standing aside, I watched the valet lift the old Duke from the coach, heavy blanket and all, and after placing him into his wheelchair, push him up the walk toward the door. I followed silently behind. Even the valet was dressed in a fine navy blue uniform tonight.

When we reached the door, the valet gave our invitation to the man at the entrance who took our cloaks and we took our place in a long line of people waiting to be announced. I scanned the room eagerly to see what the other women were wearing. I had to admit, no one had on a more beautiful gown than the lovely green one the Duke's son had gifted to me. I noticed the Duke wore a stark white shirt with an expertly tied cravat. His navy blue coat boasted his crest on the lapel pocket and he wore a heavy golden ring upon his left hand, which also bore his ducal crest.

"Rockford, there is no need for me to wait in this line. Move me to the front," the Duke instructed his attendant. Then facing me, the Duke said, "One of the many benefits of my title." I forced a grin.

The valet pushed the Duke's chair to the front of the long line. The Duke took my hand in his. "You look lovely, my dear, but why do you fidget so? Smile. Once we are announced, every eye will fall upon you, and you are sure to capture many a man's heart this night."

There was only one man's heart I was interested in capturing. I felt the Duke's touch upon my wrist as he fingered the silver bracelet. But before he could comment, they announced our arrival.

"His Grace, Wentworth Simmons, The Duke of Devonshire, escorting The Lady Catherine Nettleton." We proceeded into the room, the Duke being pushed in his chair by his valet and me walking nervously by his side. A hush fell over the crowd and every eye turned toward us. I couldn't help but notice the heads of some of the women coming together, whispering behind gloved hands. As we passed, I overheard one say, "She's young enough to be his granddaughter. Shameless." *Gossips*, I thought, and felt the heat rise to my cheeks in spite of my attempt to maintain a cool resolve.

The Duke directed the valet to wheel him toward the set of French doors that opened out onto a veranda. I stood beside him wringing my hands, feeling very much out of place and not knowing quite what to do. Soft strains of music played, and I forced myself to concentrate on hearing it above the hum of voices in conversation, which grew louder in anticipation of the arrival of the guests of honor. The hum reminded me of the horrible evening of Blackbeard's auction, and I compelled myself to squelch those memories.

Finally, the heroes' names were announced, and I held my breath, my eyes riveted on the entrance. The Governor of the Colony of Virginia entered first, accompanied by his wife, a plain and mousy-looking woman with pale skin and dark beady eyes. Following him were the two men who were instrumental in the capture of the notorious Blackbeard, Robert Maynard and Edmund Drake.

I felt my jaw drop open when they were introduced as Lieutenants in the Royal Navy. My heart pounded rapidly against my breast and I felt slightly lightheaded. Edmund was not a pirate after all. His eloquent manners and speech suddenly made sense. But why pretend to be a pirate?

Both men were dressed in the navy blue formal uniform of their rank and around each of their necks a medal hung on a thick pale blue ribbon. At first I did not realize I was staring with my mouth gaping open, until Rockford nudged me and I clamped my jaw closed, clenching my teeth. *What else do I not know about you? What other secrets do you have, Edmund Drake?*

Robert and Edmund stopped at the foot of the stairs, where people starting gathering and formed a receiving line.

"Come my dear, allow me to introduce you to Edmund." The valet pushed the Duke's wheel chair forward ahead of the throng, and I followed silently, not quite knowing how this would play out. We approached Edmund and my stomach turned into a ball of knots. I thought for certain I would be ill. The Duke introduced me to the governor and his mouse of a wife, Anne, and then to Lieutenant Maynard, whose eyes smiled brightly as he took in my appearance. Finally I reached Edmund.

I felt hot and cold at the same time. The knot in my stomach moved up to my throat and thought I would vomit. My palms were sweaty and I felt lightheaded. The sounds of the room seemed to melt away and all I could see was Edmund's handsome face, his smile, his green eyes twinkling with amusement.

"Who is this lovely vision you have managed to ensnare, Your Grace?" Edmund asked.

"This beautiful woman is Lady Catherine Nettleton, Countess of Dorset, soon to be the Duchess of Devonshire. Catherine, my dear, this is-"

"I am Edmund Drake, Milady, and it is truly a pleasure to make your acquaintance." He took my trembling hand and brought my fingers to his lips. Our eyes met as he placed a soft kiss upon my fingertips and my knees got weak. My heart thundered and I feared the entire room would hear it. The memory of his touch and his kiss brought a pool of deep desire to my lower regions and my breath quickened with it. I forced myself to focus on controlling my rapid breathing lest my heaving bosom draw attention. The sound of my blood rushing in my ears made me dizzy and I feared I would swoon from it.

Finding my voice, I managed, "Thank you, Lieutenant Drake, for ridding us of a truly dangerous pirate and making our waters safe once again. I believe I read you have been chasing the blackguard around the waters of the Caribbean for a few years."

"Yes, that is true, Milady. I did chase him and although I did not deliver the fatal blow, my crew was instrumental in positioning him and allowing for his capture and ultimate death."

I was overcome with a sadness I didn't quiet expect at the thought of Blackbeard's death. I could hardly believe the fierce and vibrant man was no longer alive. And what had happened to the Contessa, the dear, dear Contessa?

"Perhaps you would allow me to tell you of my adventures sometime." The timbre of Edmund's deep voice sounded like music to my ears and drew me out of my sorrow.

"Perhaps."

"I promise you will be quite entertained with tales of my crew climbing rigging and dancing their jigs upon the deck of my ship."

Heat swamped my body and pooled between my legs as memories of Edmund aboard the *The Lady Victoria* bombarded me. *Was his mention of climbing rigging and dancing on deck designed by him to seek an effect?* I dared not utter a sound lest he realize then that he had succeeded.

"At the very least, perhaps you will honor me with a dance this night?"

"Perhaps," I whispered, hoping the Duke hadn't noticed the breathless quality of my voice. From Edmund's darkening gaze, I knew he'd heard the lingering need so apparent to my ears.

His intense gaze held mine and I felt weak when his fingers slid to my wrist, certain he would feel my pulse race at his touch. "What a lovely and unique bracelet. Dare I say its beauty pales in comparison to yours?"

"You flatter me, Lieutenant. How kind of you to notice. It was a gift given to me a long time ago."

"And yet you wear it still. It must be dear to you."

"Yes, it is. Now if you would kindly excuse us, I fear those behind us grow impatient," I said, easing my fingers from his grasp.

"I look forward to having the opportunity to speak with you later, Milady."

I don't know how I managed to walk away from him since I could hardly feel my legs.

"Edmund seems quite taken with you, my dear."

Fear prickled across my scalp. I dare not let my true feeling show lest I endanger both Edmund and me. *The Duke may be wheelchair bound, but* . . . I swallowed and pasted a fake smile across my lips.

"I doubt he has any interest in me, Your Grace," I replied. I feared revealing my true feelings to the Duke. "Men like Edmund Drake would not think of me as more than someone to pass idle time with until called off to his next adventure."

The Duke grinned. "Is that what you think? Why, any man would find you attractive and most interesting, I assure you, and I would imagine Edmund would not be immune to your charm and beauty."

"Thank you, Your Grace. You do flatter me."

The music began and he said, "I'm afraid I cannot dance with you, my dear. However, if you should be invited to dance, and I am certain you will be, please feel free to accept any invitation you wish. I want you to enjoy the ball."

I smiled, but fully intended to stand beside him the remainder of the evening. A role I would fill until he, or I, passed from this world. My chest constricted at the thought and I found it difficult to draw a breath.

I spotted Edmund striding toward the musicians. After having a brief conversation, he turned and headed directly toward me as the strain of a familiar tune began to play. My heart skipped several beats and my breath caught. They were playing the waltz we danced to that night aboard *The Lady Victoria*.

My eyes never wavered as I watched him approach me. He inclined his head toward the Duke, who indicated his permission by giving a short nod.

"Countess, would you honor me with the pleasure of this dance?"

I glanced at the Duke, whose smile crinkled the edges of his kind, knowing eyes. "Go on, my dear. Enjoy."

Edmund took my hand and drew me out onto the dance floor and into his embrace. Memories of our dance on deck that night swirled through my mind. I trembled in his arms, but I could not help it.

"You look ravishing this evening, Milady," he whispered as he drew me closer. His words glided on heated breath around my ear. I longed to lean into his hard chest, to feel the heat of him molding me to him. I knew every eye in the room was on me, watching, waiting for me to slip up and betray the Duke. I knew what the gossips would have to say.

They were already whispering behind their fans and gloved hands. I didn't know if I could control my yearning to be in Edmund's arms, but I knew I had to try.

"Thank you, Lieutenant," I said with a heavy emphasis upon his rank.

He chuckled. "I'm sorry I could not tell you of my purpose."

"What else do I not know about you?" I could hardly think. All I wanted was to be closer to him, but I dared not press my body against him in such a public forum. His arm tightened around me ever so slightly, but in that one movement, I knew he too wanted more. My fingers trembled in his warm hand and I ached with a deep need.

"It would take me years to tell you, perhaps the remainder of my days, yet I would gladly take the time should you allow it." His green eyes darkened as he gazed down into mine. I instantly recalled that look of longing in his stare.

"I'm sure you could find more interesting ways to pass your idle time until your next mission." When I uttered the word 'mission' I painfully recalled Mister Smith's words admonishing Edmund to remember the mission on that day we'd picnicked on the deserted island.

The deep, rich laughter that erupted from him shook me. He pulled me shamelessly close. "Do you recall the first time we danced to this song, Catherine?" he whispered against my ear.

All too aware of our spectators, I planted my hand against his chest and attempted to put more space between us. I had no doubt every available woman watched the most handsome man in the room dance with the Duke's intended. "Have we danced to this song? Pity, but I cannot recall it." I averted my gaze, focusing instead on the grand staircase before he adeptly swirled me to the beat of the music.

"You are not a convincing liar, Countess."

"Oh, but you are, Lieutenant."

"Edmund. Say my name." He tightened his arms around me.

I could hardly breathe. "You take inappropriate liberties by holding me so closely. I am to be married to the Duke, as you well know, Lieutenant."

A shadow crossed his face, but was quickly replaced by a look I had come to associate with desire. He lowered his lips to my ear. "I have held you closer. Perhaps you recall the day you soaked my clothes when I lifted you from your bath?"

My cheeks burned. How could I forget? I had relived that moment every night since, re-experiencing sensual sensations . . . wondering what it would have been like if we hadn't been interrupted, if he could have done to me what I'd witnessed Blackbeard doing to the Contessa. The way that at one point Blackbeard had trailed kisses down the Contessa's body, then did something I couldn't see, but could only imagine. The room suddenly grew warm and I grew dizzy with emotion. "I-I have tried to forget it."

"I cannot forget that or anything else about you." Edmund's gaze burned into me and my heart fluttered. *Dare I have a hope? Steel yourself . . . you must not falter . . . you are not free to think such thoughts.*

"You cannot say such things, Lieutenant. Have you forgotten? I am to be married. You must forget me."

"Nay, Milady, take pity on me for I have tried."

He swung me toward the veranda door. "Would you care for some fresh air?" he asked, sweeping me out onto the terrace and into the darkness.

The strains of the waltz drifted out through the opened doors just as the light from the room spilled out onto the stone veranda. Taking my hand, he led me toward a darkened corner. Although it was nearly winter, and the night grew cold, a rush of heat flooded me when he drew me into his arms. My heart thundered and I felt my legs were about to give out beneath me. But, before I could react, he lowered his lips to mine.

Chapter 31

Lady Catherine

Edmund's lips covered mine in a possessiveness I didn't know existed, a possessiveness I only hoped he would have for me. Despite myself, I responded to his kiss. My hand rested over his heart and my other entwined in his hair. His lips devoured mine, revealing a hunger, a need boiling just beneath the surface that seemed barely within control. *Was I dreaming or was this real?* I had wanted this for so long.

The smell of him, soap and leather and man, made me drunk with the same hunger, wanton with the same need. I leaned into him, unable to resist. He ran his hand down my back and drew me up against him. I felt the hardness of his body against mine and my heart skipped a beat. I wanted to be naked in his arms once again, but at the back of my mind, I realized that the music had changed. The waltz had ended. The Duke would be looking for me and many eyes had followed us out here.

Drawing on a strength I did not know I possessed, I pulled away from Edmund.

"What are you thinking? You'll get us both killed," I whispered. Picking up the lush fabric of my gown, I hurried back into the great hall and made my way to stand beside the Duke.

"Is everything all right, my dear?" he asked, his feeble voice a hair above a whisper.

"Everything is fine, Your Grace. Why do you ask?"

"Your face is flushed and you seem breathless."

"Please accept my apologies, Your Grace, but it is the dance. I am not accustomed to such lively frivolity."

My heart stopped when he glanced at the door just in time to see Edmund's return. "I understand completely, my dear," the old man murmured.

True to the prediction of the old Duke, I was indeed asked to dance by many a young swain. Not wanting to single Edmund out as my sole partner, I accepted each offer and graced each gentleman with my most brilliant of smiles. As expected, I lightly flirted, appearing to hang attentively on their every word, and when I chanced a glance toward Edmund, I found his dark gaze watching me through hooded eyes. He leaned lazily against the wall with a brooding expression, and I knew from experience his mood was dangerous. Although many attractive women stared hopefully in his direction, he ignored them.

A stab of fear caught in my throat. Did he not understand that if I could see he had eyes for no one else in the room that the gossips would take notice and so too, the Duke? But I had no manner in which to warn him.

After being swirled around the room by my latest devotee, who stepped on my toes at least three times, I was relieved when the music ended and I rejoined the Duke.

"I am delighted to see you having such a wonderful evening, but I grow tired, my dear, and fear I must take my leave."

I peered closer, noting the lines of fatigue slating across his pale cheeks.

"I apologize, Your Grace, for keeping you so long. Let us get our wraps."

"No, no, my dear. There is no need for you to miss out on the party. You may stay if you wish."

"Your Grace, that would be terribly inappropriate. I could not remain here unescorted."

"Sorry for the intrusion, Your Grace." Edmund's deep voice sent a spiral of dread along my spine. "I could not help but overhear your conversation. If you must depart, I would be honored to escort Lady Catherine and return her to her home. I am completely at your disposal."

What was he thinking? The Duke was no fool. I tried to warn Edmund with my eyes, but he seemed amused at my efforts. I forced a polite smile. "Thank you, Lieutenant. That's very kind of you but that won't be necessary. I shall be leaving with His Grace."

"Nonsense, my dear, you should remain here with the young people and enjoy yourself. I trust Lieutenant Drake will be quite the gentleman. Isn't that correct, Lieutenant?"

Something I didn't understand passed between the two men and Edmund nodded. "Of course."

Edmund held out his hand. "Milady, as His Grace has so aptly pointed out, I am a gentleman and have promised to behave as such."

"I arrived with the Duke, and it is only proper that I should now leave with him," I answered.

The Duke raised his white bushy eyebrows.

"Lieutenant Drake, please escort Lady Catherine. See to it she has a wonderful and most memorable evening and that she gets home safely."

"You may count on me, Your Grace," Edmund replied.

Turning to his valet the Duke said, "Rockford, if you would kindly call for the coach."

Placing his hand upon my arm, Edmund said, "Milady, I hear the strains of a waltz beginning. Come. Let us enjoy this dance."

"I find I am tired," I replied, easing my arm from his grasp.

Placing my hand upon the old Duke's shoulder, I walked beside him as Rockford pushed the rickety wooden chair, hoping against hope the Duke would rescind his decree and allow me to slip away with him. As we approached the door, I felt Edmund's warm hand upon my shoulder.

"Milady?" Edmund whispered.

I stood stone still, trying to will myself to move forward.

The Duke raised his eyes to me. His shoulders slumped and his thin skin had a gray pallor to it. He nodded. "Go, my dear. Have a lovely time. I must retire now."

Once again, I had no choice. "Good evening, Your Grace. Thank you so much for allowing me the honor of accompanying you. I have had a delightful evening." I bent down and placed a soft kiss upon his wrinkled cheek.

He took my hand into his gnarled grasp. "It is I who have been honored, my dear. Enjoy the remainder of the evening. Edmund, promise me you will take good care of Lady Catherine. She is a very special woman," the old Duke said as he placed my hand into Edmund's.

"I shall, Your Grace. You have my vow."

I watched Rockford secure the heavy blanket over the Duke's legs and push him out into the lightly falling snow to the waiting coach, leaving me alone with Edmund.

Chapter 32

Lady Catherine

"Come, Milady, allow me to escort you back into the hall," Edmund said, taking hold of my arm and leading me back into the party.

I stiffened my spine and my resolve, which I vowed not to allow him to weaken.

"Would you care for some refreshment, Lady Catherine?"

"No, thank you, Lieutenant."

"Very well then, would you care to dance?"

"No, thank you." I held myself rigid.

"Come, let us find a seat," he said sternly. He held out his arm and, aware of all the envious stares, I accepted and allowed him to guide me toward a plush settee. The location offered a splendid view of the couples whirling around the dance floor. I took a good amount of time straightening my gown and purposely made no eye contact with him, nor did I utter a word. I made certain my skirts took up the entire seat to be sure there would not be sufficient room for him to sit beside me. He said nothing but took his place, standing behind the settee.

No sooner had I gotten comfortable, when a young handsome gentleman approached. His honey-colored hair was neatly tied back and his dark eyes twinkled with a suppressed smile. The cut of his coat suggested he had wealth and perhaps even title.

"Good evening, Milady," he said.

"Good evening," I said, swallowing nervously as Edmund placed his hand possessively upon my shoulder.

"I am Sir Geoffrey Kent, and I wonder if you would honor me with this dance? That is, of course, if the Lieutenant would not mind."

Ignoring his reference to Edmund and placing my hand in his, I replied, "It is I who would be honored, Sir Geoffrey."

I rose and allowed him to whisk me out onto the dance floor. As we moved around the room, I dared a glance toward Edmund and when my eyes met his, I nearly gasped aloud. His green eyes had grown dark and fierce, his jaw tightened, and his hands fisted by his sides. When his gaze met mine, he appeared to relax, though I suspected he did so only for my benefit.

I turned my focus to conversation with Sir Geoffrey. Allowing him my full attention, I laughed at his humorous comments but all too soon the dance came to an end, and he escorted me back to my seat.

"It has been a pleasure to meet you, Sir Geoffrey, and thank you for the dance."

"The pleasure has truly been mine, Milady. Perhaps you would allow me to dance with you again."

"Perhaps," I said in my sweetest voice and graced him with a brilliant smile.

After making brief conversation with Edmund and a few polite exchanges, Sir Geoffrey quickly slipped away.

The strains of another waltz began, and Edmund took my hand. Pulling me to my feet, he took me into his arms and whisked me onto the dance floor.

"Lieutenant, you presume far too much," I said, fearful my body would betray me again. This wouldn't do at all. How could others miss this, this *energy* that seemed to build whenever the two of us drew close?

"Milady?"

"I have no desire to dance with you."

"Of course not." He urged me closer into his embrace, and the heat of his strong body melted into mine. The scent of him disarmed my senses, and memories of his kisses flooded me with a rush of liquid lightening. A tingle ran down my spine at the feel of his hand upon my back. I wanted to feel his hands on my naked skin, to feel the tingle of his touch on my breasts, and in my most private places. Struggling, I drew myself out of my fantasy.

"Lieutenant, you hold me far too close and are sure to cause a scandal."

"Milady, I care little for the gossip of dowagers and spinsters."

"Aren't you fearful for your life? The Duke could have you killed."

"I wouldn't blame him, either. When Sir Geoffrey held you, I wanted to rip him apart with my bare hands. Why should he get to hold you when I cannot?" He trailed a finger along the edge of my shoulder. "Touch you when I cannot?"

I could hardly breathe. "Lieutenant, you truly are a scoundrel."

"Every Lady needs a scoundrel in her life."

His gaze traveled over my bosom. My breasts swelled and the tips hardened under the heat of his stare. I tried to hold myself the proper distance from him, but my body betrayed me as I leaned into his embrace.

His breathing quickened, becoming shallow.

Two can play this game, Edmund. "What is wrong, Lieutenant?"

"Not a thing, Milady," he whispered. "Not a thing in the world."

I ran my hand along the expanse of his shoulder, then brushed my breasts against his chest, drawing my already sensitive tips into peaks.

He seemed to be holding his breath and as he dipped me forward then back, I felt the length of his arousal pressing against his uniform.

I swallowed hard, knowing we were playing a dangerous game, one I couldn't seem to compel myself to end. All I could think of was lying naked in his arms, spreading myself as the Contessa had, allowing Edmund to thrust his hardness into me the way . . . As another rush of heat washed over me, I knew I had to stop lest we start the place on fire. But I did not want to stop. I wanted to feel the fire burn between us. One glance around the room confirmed my guess that every eye was upon me. I had to get control of this situation. I had to say something to distract Edmund and lead him into a conversation.

"L-lovely evening, isn't it, Lieutenant? You know I just now realized I never had the opportunity to thank you for rescuing me from the auction." I offered him my most charming smile.

"You are certainly welcome, Milady." His gaze softened. "Did the black heart . . ."

I watched his Adam's apple bob up and down in swift, sharp motion.

". . . hurt you?"

I shook my head. "No. I never feared Captain Teach. He was kind to me."

A look of relief passed across his face before his features hardened again. "You consider being auctioned off to the highest bidder to be an act of kindness?"

"Certainly not. What I meant to say is that he never . . . compromised me in any way."

"You were lucky, Milady. Rumor has it he passed his wife around among his crew, after which, she mysteriously disappeared."

The music ended and we stopped, waiting for the next song to begin, both of us oblivious to those around us.

"I spent most of my time with the Contessa and I wonder now what has become of her."

"She's quite safe, I assure you."

"You know, she instructed me"—I leaned slightly closer and whispered against his neck, right below his ear—"in the art of pleasuring a man." My warm breath sailed along his neck, and goose flesh rose on his skin in its wake.

"Instructed? How?"

I forced back a grin at the hoarse quality of his voice.

"She taught me many, many things," I cooed. "She actually had me watch her and Captain Teach make love. Have you ever . . . watched, Lieutenant?" I asked, soft and slow, just as the Contessa had taught me.

He held me tightly in his arms and seemed to be holding his breath. "Nay," he replied, his voice a husky whisper.

"She also taught me how to do some amazing things to a man's body . . . with my tongue." My breath caressed his ear. "You must allow me to tell you of them sometime."

I was behaving scandalously, but I couldn't help myself. His body stiffened, and I knew my words were having the effect I desired.

He smiled then and whispered against my ear, "Milady, I must warn you, should you continue along this path, I may ravish you right here on this dance floor."

"Whatever are you talking about, Lieutenant?" I whispered. The band started playing another waltz, and the hand he had rested upon my waist slid slightly upward, where his knuckles brushed the edge of my breast. I couldn't hold in the gasp of unexpected pleasure.

"Lieutenant, need I remind you of your vow to the Duke that you would behave as a gentleman?" I whispered.

He said nothing, but only smiled.

Before I realized it, he swirled us toward an archway, then grasped my hand and strode purposefully down a dimly lit hallway away from the crowded ballroom. Many oak doors lined the hallway and shoving one of them open, he dragged me into a darkened room and closed the door behind us. Without a word, he planted my back against the heavy wooden door. His lips found mine in a desperate, urgent kiss. Leaning his body against mine, he held me there as one of his hands cupped my breast. My heart thundered and damp heat rushed to my core. My blood pounded in my ears, and I was breathless from the passion in his kiss. My arms wound around his neck, and I clung to him as his urgency also became mine. Lifting my skirts, he ran his hand up my thigh. He moved aside my undergarments and his fingers found the center of my womanhood. I gasped when he slid one into me. I felt my body clamp around him, felt my moisture on his finger as he withdrew, then entered me again. Although I had seen this when watching the Contessa, I had no idea how wonderful it would feel. And I wanted more. I moved my hips to draw his fingers deeper into my aching wetness. But it wasn't enough. I wanted to feel the length of him inside me and I was ablaze with desire for him.

My hands burned to touch his flesh and with frantic fingers I unbuttoned first his coat and then his shirt.

Pushing the material of my bodice aside, he freed my breast. I thought I would burst when he teased my nipple with his fingers. Dragging his lips from mine, he bent his head and drew my erect nipple slowly into his mouth as he continued to torment me beneath my skirt.

"Edmund," I whispered in a hoarse voice I didn't even recognize.

He did not answer me, but moved his mouth back to mine, and my tongue danced with his. I ran my hand down his hard chest, down along his flat stomach, until my fingers caressed the hardness of him.

A moan escaped him as I rubbed him through the material of his trousers.

"Catherine, my love," he whispered, pulling his lips away from mine, "I want you right here, right now."

My lips found his chest, and I circled my tongue around his nipple even as my fingers continued to caress his hard shaft. A groan came from deep within him as I sucked his nipple into my mouth . . . slowly.

His fingers moved faster as they rubbed against my wetness, and my hips moved in time with his touch. I pressed myself wantonly against his palm as an unfamiliar pressure built inside of me. I became frantic with a need to feel him fill me, to end the sweet torment.

My breathing grew as rapid as his, but when I was finally able to unfasten his trousers, freeing his swollen manhood and taking it into my hand, a fierce growl rumbled from his chest.

He went rigid and stilled his fingers, and I knew he was struggling for control. Not wanting him to find it, I stroked his erection. The Contessa's instructions raced through my mind, and I drew my lips down his nipple and allowed my tongue to leave a wet trail down to his navel. I delighted in the exploration of his taut, muscular body. But when my wet tongue ran up the length of his erect shaft, his breath caught in his throat.

I slowly drew the tip of his hardness into my warm, wet mouth, sucking slowly as my hand continued to massage the length of him.

"Good God, woman," he whispered.

His body trembled as I continued to run my tongue slowly over the head. Letting the tip of my tongue slip over the opening, I flirted with the first salty taste of his essence that appeared in a tiny shimmering drop. A fierce growl erupted from him as he grabbed me and lifted, forcing me to release his throbbing shaft, pinning me against the door and bringing his lips to mine. With one hand under my bum, he lifted me and held me to him. I drew my legs up around his waist and prepared to receive his manhood.

"Edmund, please," I whispered, trembling with need as I clung to his shoulders.

With his other hand, he guided his hard shaft toward me and rubbed up against my slick wetness. When he deliberately ran it across my throbbing pearl, I nearly exploded.

"Catherine, my love. I fear I cannot stop," he whispered into his kiss.

"Edmund, I do not want you to stop."

"Are you certain?"

I moved my hips, causing my soft wet womanhood to glide over the tip of his hardness.

He growled through gritted teeth and guided his shaft into me.

I clung to his shoulders, drunk with the sensation of my nipples rubbing against his hard, naked chest, his tongue dancing with mine, his warm hand upon my bottom, the thickness of his hard manhood easing into me.

After a brief stab of pain, I drove my hips forward to meet his. I reveled in the sensation of the length of him filling me. He moved slowly, and I met his every thrust. I thought I would burst in a flood of release when his fingers found my tender and throbbing bud.

Nothing existed for me at that moment . . . nothing but Edmund and the fire burning between us. His pace quickened as did the pressure of his fingers against my swollen pearl. Panting for breath, my heart thundering, my body shaking, he drove himself deep in one final thrust and I felt his release explode deep inside of me, pushing me over the edge. I could hold back no longer. I came crashing down into the pool of my own release. And I cried out when that release came. Waves of sheer ecstasy washed over me, and I was drowning in a flood of pleasure I never wanted to be rescued from.

He clutched me to him. "Catherine, I . . ."

I gazed up at him through hooded eyes, lazy with the afterglow of being ravished.

"Yes, Edmund?"

"I . . . I didn't want the first time between us to be like this. I wanted it to be perfect."

"It was perfect."

"I promise you, the next time it shall be. I want to taste every inch of your glorious body. Catherine, I-"

"Lieutenant Drake?" a man's voice called from somewhere down the hallway, followed by the faint sound of a knock, and footsteps drawing closer to the door indicated his approach.

My heart thundered as I shoved urgently against Edmund's chest, while struggling to straighten the bodice of my gown. What would happen if we got caught?

"Lieutenant Drake?" the voice sounded closer.

I lowered my legs from around him and dropped my hem into place with trembling fingers. "Edmund, hurry, someone is looking for you, and we must not be discovered like this," I whispered.

Edmund adjusted his clothes and I ran fingers through my hair.

"Shh," he whispered. "Allow him to pass the room and when we are certain he has gone, we shall slip out and return to the ballroom."

He crushed me against him, and I buried my face into his shirt and held my breath.

"Lieutenant Drake?"

The voice sounded just outside of the room, and there was a soft knock on the door I prayed would stay closed. I feared whoever was on the other side of that door had heard me cry out and would now surely hear my thundering heart. But the footsteps moved away from the door and echoed on down the hall. We stood there in silence, my legs trembling. Finally Edmund drew slightly away from me.

"Catherine, I'm going to open the door to be sure the hallway is clear. If it is, allow me to go out. You follow after a few moments have passed. Do you understand?" he whispered.

"Yes," I answered, swallowing hard. The thought of the danger of being caught in this compromising position made my pulse race and I clung to him.

"Edmund, do something for me," I whispered.

"Anything, my love."

"Kiss me."

His lips took mine, but unlike the passion that had ripped though us mere moments ago, his kiss was gentle and held the tenderness of a promise. Our lips parted and before I knew what had happened, Edmund had slipped out the door and disappeared into the hallway.

Chapter 33

The remainder of the evening was a blur. All I could think about was Edmund and the fierce desire he had ignited in me. The strains of music became a vague memory to me now sitting beside him in his coach. Light snow continued to fall, and its chill had permeated the coach. Despite the fact that he had wrapped me tightly in my cloak, a shiver ran over me and, much to my surprise, he pulled me onto his lap.

"Edmund!" I gasped.

"You are cold, my love. Allow me to warm you," he whispered, cradling me in his arms.

I snuggled into his embrace and rested my head against his shoulder, welcoming the warmth that radiated from him. His soft kiss played upon my hair. Did he just call me his love? My heart fluttered at his words. I lifted my face to his, and his soft lips found mine. His kiss was gentle, and he placed his hand beside my jaw. I could let him kiss me like this for the remainder of my days.

He drew his lips from mine and holding my face now between his hands, he stared deeply into my eyes.

My heart nearly burst with love for him, and despite what had happened between us, I could not tell him of it, for in a matter of weeks, I would be married to the Duke. As the coach pulled up before the elegant house I temporarily called home, I was overcome with a sadness so profound I could not find my voice.

Lifting me from the coach, he held me against him for a long moment.

"Edmund, why do you not you set me down?" I whispered.

"Milady, there is snow here. Allow me to carry you to the door so you do not spoil your gown."

He did not wait for me to answer but turned and made his way to the house. James opened the door and light flooded our path as we neared the entrance.

"Good evening, Milord, Milady," James uttered.

"Good evening, James. It is a pleasure to see you," Edmund said.

"When we received word you would be in London, I wondered if we would be seeing you here at Hartington House."

I looked from James to Edmund. "You two know each other?"

"Yes, James and I go way back. He's been like a father to me, and we have quite a history here at Hartington House, don't we, James?" Edmund replied, but offered no further information.

He set me down in the foyer and after removing my cloak handed it to the butler.

"How do you find your accommodations here, Milady?" Edmund asked.

"My rooms are beautiful."

"I am happy to hear that. I understand the Marquis had them designed specifically with you in mind."

"Surely you are mistaken, Lieutenant, as I have yet to meet him."

"Nay, Milady, of this I am certain."

"Do you know the Marquis of Hartington, Lieutenant?"

"Extremely well, Milady."

"Perhaps one day you could introduce me to him."

"Perhaps."

"It's dreadfully cold, Lieutenant, would you care to come in for some tea, or perhaps a sip of brandy before you leave?" I asked, fearful I would not see him again and hoping to prolong our time together.

"Thank you, Milady, but I should be on my way before the weather worsens."

"I understand. Thank you, Lieutenant, for escorting me and seeing me home safely in the Duke's stead."

"It has truly been my pleasure, Milady. I shall see you again before you wed the Duke."

His words cut through me. He had made love to me, yet he still expected me to marry the Duke.

"Perhaps." My heart ached so at his words that my voice rose barely above a whisper.

"I would very much like to finish the spirited contest we began this evening."

"I do not know if that would be possible, Lieutenant."

"Not only will it be possible, Milady, but were I you, I would count on it."

The sting of color flushed my cheeks.

"And now, sadly, I must depart. But I shall not be far. I shall call upon you tomorrow, if that would be all right."

I stood in the foyer of the grand mansion momentarily stunned. "Yes, certainly, Lieutenant."

"James," Edmund said and nodded toward the butler.

"Good evening, Milord."

"Good evening, Milady," Edmund said to me.

"Lieutenant," I replied.

Then, much to my surprise and despite the fact that the butler stood watching, he leaned closer and kissed me.

I pressed my fingers to my lips while he swept out of the front door and into the night.

"Miss, how was the celebration? Was that Captain Drake?" Mary came bounding down the stairs and rushed to my side.

"The celebration was joyful and yes, that was Captain Drake."

"I was o' the mind ye would be delivered home by the Duke."

"As was I, Mary, but the Duke grew overly tired and wished to retire early. He left Captain Drake to escort me home. You will never believe what I have discovered, Mary. The Captain was never a pirate."

"No! Well, that explains his gentlemanly ways an' the aristocratic air wot he gots about him."

"He is actually a Lieutenant in the Royal Navy and posed as a pirate in a ruse to capture Blackbeard."

"Ye don't say."

"You do not seem surprised."

"Nay, Miss. Tobias confided in me."

"Tobias knew this?"

"Aye, me Lady."

"And he told you?"

"Aye, Miss."

"Yet you saw fit to keep that information from me?"

"Aye, there were no point in tellin' ye since we was already here."

"I see. What else has Tobias told you about Lieutenant Drake that you are keeping from me?"

"Miss, wot makes ye think I be keepin' things from ye? Now come, ye must be cold. There be a warm fire in yer room, and I be bringin' ye some hot cocoa. We don't be wantin' ye to catch your death now, do we?"

Mary was so like a mother to me, and I smiled as I followed her up the stairs.

As promised, the fire was burning in the huge hearth, and the room was toasty warm. Mary placed the cup of hot cocoa on the bedside table and helped me out of my gown to ready me for bed. She held up my bloodied and soiled undergarments. "Me Lady, I don't mean to be oversteppin' me place, but be there somethin' ye be wantin' to tell me?"

Fire burned in my cheeks, and lowering my gaze, I burst into tears.

"Now, now, Miss. No need to get yerself all in tears." She crossed the short distance between us and wrapped me in a hug.

"Oh, Mary, I have made such a mess of things," I sobbed.

"He's done it, then. He's stolen yer virtue."

"Oh, no. It wasn't like that at all."

"No? How was it then? Did ye attack him 'n force him to take that wot don't rightly belong to him?"

I sobbed heavily now.

"Oh, Mary. What have I done? How can I present myself to the Duke as an untouched maiden now, when it's a lie?"

"Oh, now, Miss, perhaps the old Duke won't have his wits about him enough to notice."

"He would notice, Mary. Look at the soiled mess of the garment in your hand. How would the lack thereof possibly go unnoticed? Besides, there isn't going to be a wedding."

"Wot ye be sayin', Miss?"

"Everything I am belongs to Edmund; my mind, heart, body, even my soul. Tomorrow I shall tell the Duke the wedding is off."

"Oh, now, Miss, wot of yer father? Ain't he countin' on the marriage wot to cure his, er, financial situation?"

"Yes." I sighed.

"Then ye best think on this, me Lady. Ye best keep mum on the matter. Marriage to the Duke won't be so bad an' by the look o' the ol' goat, probably won't be long before ye be a widow. Then mayhap ye can be o' the mind to marry for love. Don't ye be frettin' on it none. There be ways to cover yer indiscretions. No one need be the wiser."

After she left the room, I slipped into bed and snuggled down under the warm comforter, memories of swirling waltzes and passionate encounters stirring in my mind. I glanced at the cup of hot cocoa, but left it untouched as I drifted off to sleep. My dreams that night were a continuation of my encounter with Edmund in the darkened room at the ball.

When I woke in the morning, the room was still warm. Sighing deeply, I reached for the cup of cocoa, but it was gone.

I sat up in the bed and looked around the room. A fire burned softly in the hearth and the cup of cocoa sat upon the table next to the armchair before the fire. The chair, however, no longer faced the fire, but rather faced the bed. Pushing the covers aside, I rose from the bed and made my way sleepily toward the chair.

I wondered how my cocoa got over here, and when I looked in the cup I found it to be empty. *Well, I hope the ghost who visited my room last night enjoyed my cocoa.*

Mary bustled into the room then and she seemed in a hurry.

"Good morning, Mary." I stretched and yawned.

"Miss, ye must hurry an' get dressed." She stood beside the dressing table wringing her hands.

"What is it, Mary? What has happened?" My first thought was that somehow the Duke had discovered what had happened between Edmund and me.

"It be the Duke, Miss."

Were my worst fears about to be realized?

"Has he arrived already? It's a bit early for him to be calling." I tried to sound as if my heart were not thundering in my throat.

"Nay, Miss, he ain't come callin', and I would venture to guess he ain't never goin' to."

"Good Lord, Mary, has he discovered . . .?" I couldn't even bring myself to utter the words. Had our reckless behavior endangered our lives?

She took a tentative step toward me, and the color drained from her cheeks as she stood there still wringing her hands.

"For heaven's sake, Mary. What has happened?" A cold dread rushed over me, and the hair on my neck rose. I lowered my voice. "Is it Edmund?"

"Miss, it be awful. The Duke, well, he be no longer with us."

"What? What do you mean 'he's no longer is with us'?"

"I mean . . . the ol' Duke . . . well, he died last night, in his sleep they say."

I stood there in disbelief. I had no feelings of love for the old man, but still I was overcome by the thought that the man who had shown me kindness, and that I'd been about to marry, had died.

"I'm so sorry, Miss."

"Oh, Mary. This is dreadful."

"Aye, Miss. Wot'll ever become of us now?"

Chapter 34

At the funeral, Lieutenant Drake took charge and acted as if he were some relation. Everyone who shook his hand and spoke to him in soft whispers seemed sincere in their condolences. A few came over to me, but I knew the gossips were whispering behind gloved hands.

After the funeral services, I was taken back to Hartington House in a coach with the Duke's crest upon its doors. I was numb and really did not know how I should be feeling, but despite this, I knew I had to make arrangements for our departure.

"Mary," I called from my room.

"Aye, Miss," she answered, popping her head in at the door.

"Mary, please ask Tobias to get our trunks brought up here so that we can pack."

"Pack, Miss?"

"Yes. We have been here on the good will of Duke Simmons and his son, pending the wedding, but now that the Duke has passed on, well, surely we would be expected to return to the island."

"Oh, Miss, I ain't heard no talk o' that."

"Regardless, Mary. We are already considered to have been only after the Duke's money, and I shan't allow those tongues to wag any further. We have been here on Duke Simmons' charity and that of the Marquis long enough."

"I think ye be mistaken, Miss."

"Mary, please. This is not the time to question me. Kindly ask Tobias to fetch the trunks."

"Aye, Miss." She turned and scurried out the door.

"Oh, and Mary?"

"Aye?" She popped her head back into the room.

"Did you enjoy my cocoa last night?" I tilted my head toward the empty cup, which still sat upon the table before the fire.

"Beggin' yer pardon, Miss, but it ain't me wot drunk yer cocoa."

"Is it some specter then that visits in the dark of night, turns the chair to face my bed, watches me sleep, and then drinks my cocoa?"

"I don't be knowin' nothin' 'bout no specter, Miss."

I was beginning to lose my patience. "What do you know of this?"

"Nothin', Miss. I don't be knowin' nothin'. I swear it." But she wrung her hands, and I knew she was hiding something.

My eyes narrowed. "Mary," I said in a warning tone, "I want the truth."

"I ain't got nothin' more to say on the subject."

"Very well, Mary, then please get Tobias in here with the trunks."

"Aye, Miss," she replied and hurried out of the room.

Perhaps Tobias would have something to say about the specter that had visited my bedchamber in the night.

Tobias appeared at my door with his cap in his hand and per his usual, danced from one foot to the other.

"Me Lady?"

"Tobias, would you please bring my trunks in here so that we can start packing my things?"

"Pack yer things, me Lady?"

"Yes. With the Duke having passed on, there will be no wedding. We cannot remain here on his charity or that of the Marquis."

"Well, me Lady, don't be hasty now. I be o' the mind the Marquis would be wantin' ye to remain here."

"Really? And are you acquainted with the Marquis?"

He danced again before me, then answered, "Me Lady, ye can't be leavin'. Do ye forget yer father be arrivin' in the mornin'?"

"Oh my, yes, you are right, Tobias. I had completely forgotten the Duke had sent for my father for the wedding."

"Aye, so there be no sense in preparin' to be leavin' just yet. Besides that, I have a matter o' great importance to see to tomorrow." He frowned and I wondered if he had let slip some tidbit of information he had meant to keep secret.

"And what might that be, Mister Smith?"

"Well, I-I must accompany the Captain, that is, the Lieutenant as it be, to the ceremony."

"Ceremony?"

"Aye, me Lady." He turned to leave the room.

"What ceremony, Mister Smith?"

Facing me once again, he answered, "That be the ceremony namin' the Marquis as the new Duke a Devonshire."

"I see. And who will be fetching my father at the docks?"

"Well, the Duke's son. He made all the arrangements. Ye need not worry."

"Mister Smith, does the Duke's son have a name?"

"Aye, me Lady, the Marquis a Hartington," he said and turned once more to leave the room.

"Mister Smith!" I nearly shrieked. "Where are you going now?"

"I have to get a move on. I be runnin' behind me time."

He tugged his old, red cap down over his shaggy gray hair and scurried from the room.

I nearly screamed. That man was trying my patience.

The next morning, after another night of taunting dreams and tossing and turning in sleep tormented by memories of Edmund, I made my way down to breakfast. I was surprised to see Mister Smith, standing in the hallway, hair cut and neatly combed, clean shaven, and dressed in a fine dark coat and matching trousers. He wore a clean white shirt with a neatly tied cravat and even his dark boots shown with the sparkle of a fresh shine. Mary was using a brush to be certain his coat held not a speck of lint.

"My, my, Tobias Smith. You are the picture of a gentleman dressed in your finery."

"Thank ye, me Lady." He adjusted his coat and, clearing his throat, he said, "I be pleased to make yer acquaintance."

"Very good, Mister Smith. Very good."

We laughed together just as we had that day on the ship.

I burned with the need to question the wiry little man, yet seeing the gleam in Mary's eyes as she tended to him, I thought better of it. *I will question him at length upon his return*, I thought as I made my way to the table.

But my day proved to be so full of activity with Father's arrival that thoughts of interrogating Tobias Smith completely slipped my mind.

I wanted to look just right for my father's arrival, not impoverished as we were on the island, but not dressed in an exquisite gown either. I selected a simple gown of dusty rose that had a modest neckline and long sleeves.

Father arrived in the early afternoon. We had parted under tenuous circumstances and my stomach danced with a case of the jitters as the coach drew up to the house. So not to appear to be over anxious, I hurried into the drawing room and, taking up my needlework, began to hum the tune of a song the pirates sang while they worked. I heard the commotion of the arriving coach, but I allowed James to get the door and show Father in.

I grew silent at the sound of the front door opening and that of James's deep voice greeting my father. I squeezed the needle tightly between my fingers, and my heart beat in my ears, keeping time with the ticking clock that sat on the mantel.

"Welcome to Hartington House, Milord, Milady."

Milady? What? I mindlessly drove the tip of the needle into my finger. Who on earth had Father gotten entangled with since I was taken from *The Tempest*?

"Lady Catherine is expecting you," James said. "She awaits you in the drawing room. Allow me to take your wraps." After a brief moment, he continued, "If you would kindly step this way."

The crisp rustle of skirts and staccato heels sounded. The footsteps moved closer to the drawing room, and my stomach tightened. Not quite knowing what to expect, I rose from my chair to greet my father and the woman who had accompanied him. As they entered, my mouth dropped open.

"*Bella mio*, my little'a stick, I'm so happy to see you." The Contessa's musical voice filled the room.

"Contessa? I never expected to see you again. I couldn't be happier to discover you are alive and well, and here in London."

"*Si*, it's all because of you *Captaino* Drake. He rescued me."

She spread her arms open and I rushed into her embrace. We stood together for a moment, both laughing and crying. Father remained silent as he waited patiently and watched the emotional reunion. Finally he said, "Catherine."

I turned to face him. He stood there in his brown tweed traveling clothes looking tired and for the first time I had to admit he was starting to look his age. Our eyes met and in that moment I relived all the hurt he had caused, all the times he had made me feel unimportant and like I was a burden to him. The sting of his cowardice on the day I was captured opened a new wound in my heart. Tears stung my eyes and I realized my hands were balled into fists at my side as I fought for control. Part of me wanted to kiss him and finally be accepted for who I was, and part of me wanted to kill him for always making me feel inadequate and unloved.

"Come in, come in. Please allow me to have some tea brought in." My voice sounded cold and indifferent.

James, who had been standing in the doorway simply nodded and slipped away.

"How was your journey?" I asked.

"Long," my father answered. "Truth be told, the seas are a bit rough this time of year, and I spent much of the trip feeling rather indisposed."

"Father, I thought I would never see you again,"

Why not cut right to the chase and have it out with him now?

"Catherine, I can't tell you how sorry I am."

"Sorry?"

"Yes, for that day on *The Tempest*. I should have rallied the crew and tried to do something to save you, yet I was a coward and did nothing."

"Yes, you were."

"I hope you can find it in your heart to forgive me, and then perhaps one day I shall be able to forgive myself."

Tears streamed down my cheeks. "It's not just that day, Father. You have mistreated me my entire life. You have made me feel as if I am nothing to you but a burden."

"I'm sorry." Tears pooled in his eyes. "Looking back now I think it was my way of dealing with your mother's death and I'm so sorry. I love you, Catherine. Please, can you forgive an old fool and let us start anew?"

Then my father opened his arms and all my misgivings and trepidation melted away. I rushed into his embrace.

He planted soft kisses upon my hair, and I burst into tears, releasing all the emotions I didn't even realize I had been holding back all this time. We cried together and when I glanced at the Contessa, I saw that she, too, had shed a few tears. When I was finally able to gain a measure of control, I said, "I'm so sorry to have to tell you this, Father, but I believe you have made the arduous journey for naught."

"For naught? You consider the wedding of my daughter to be naught?"

"That's just it, Father. There isn't going to be a wedding."

"No wedding?"

"Father, there is something I must tell you."

"What is it, my dear? What has happened?" A shiver rushed over him.

"Oh, where are my manners? You're cold. Please come, sit and warm yourselves by the fire." Flustered, I ushered them further into the room.

"I must admit, I have forgotten how cold it can be here in London. This frigid, damp climate can chill a man to the marrow," Father commented as he drew closer to the fire burning in the grate.

"Now, what is it you wish to tell me, Catherine?" he asked.

"Father, it's the Duke."

"What about him? Has he tried to renege on his marriage contract?"

"No, Father. It's, well, he . . ."

"Spit it out, girl."

"I don't know quite how to tell you, but the Duke has died." Despite myself, my lip quivered.

"*Madonna mio! Morto*!" The Contessa clasped her hands to her ample bosom.

"When? How did it happen?" Father asked.

"He passed in the middle of the night, in his sleep. His funeral was yesterday and Father, I have to tell you, he was a very old man."

"Surely you exaggerate. At your tender age you think me a very old man."

"No, Father, he was quite up in years."

"How old of a man was he?" he asked with a raised brow.

"He looked to be older than your father, or even his father before him. He was in a wheel chair and wheezed as he breathed. A very frail man who took to fits of coughing, and on more than one occasion I feared he would succumb to death before my very eyes."

"I knew he was somewhat older, but I had no idea. I'm sorry, Catherine."

"But he was very kind to me, as his son, the Marquis, has been. This lovely home is his son's residence, but now that the wedding will no longer occur, we should probably make arrangements to return to our home on the island."

"Please, believe me, daughter, I had no idea the Duke was so on in years when I accepted his proposal."

"I'm sure you didn't. At any rate, as I said, I fear you have traveled a very long way for naught."

Just then, Mary arrived pushing a cart holding the tea service, James following closely behind her.

"Milord," James said to my father, "this message has just been delivered for you."

"For me? But who on earth even knows I'm here?"

The cream-colored envelope had a rich look to it and was closed with a wax seal bearing the crest of the Duke of Devonshire. Tearing open the seal and removing the thin slip of paper from the envelope, Father's eyes flew over the note.

He slid his watch from the pocket in his vest and a frown crossed his brow.

"What is it, Father?"

"A request from the Marquis, the heir apparent as it were, to meet with him this afternoon. His note says there is a matter of urgency and great importance he wishes to discuss with me."

"I suspect he will be asking us to depart and leave him to his residence," I said as nerves jumped in my stomach.

"There is no way to know that for certain until I meet with him."

"What time is the meeting, Father?"

"In less than an hour's time. His note says he will be sending a coach, so if someone would kindly show me to my room, I'd best refresh my appearance and change my clothes."

"Yes, yes, of course, James will show you to your room. And, Father, I'm so sorry."

"What have you to be sorry for, Daughter?"

"That your plans seemed to have been muddled from the start."

"Do not fret, my dear. Allow me to meet with the Marquis and see what matter he thinks to be so urgent and important. We shall have plenty of time to fret after that. In the meantime, why don't you have tea and reacquaint yourself with the Contessa."

"*Si*," the Contessa said with a welcoming smile, "come, sit with me and tell me about this place you call London."

Father returned just before dinner. Although I was anxious, I allowed him time to get settled in and relax before getting into the details of his meeting with the Marquis, who by now had surely been named the new Duke of Devonshire.

I stood before the fireplace in the drawing room gazing into the flames, my mind churning with thoughts of what would become of me, of all of us. I jumped when I felt my father's hand upon my shoulder.

"Catherine, you seem troubled beyond your years," he said.

"Things have become such a mess." I turned and fell into my father's embrace.

"Father, I was beside myself with worry for you the day I was taken from *The Tempest*. How long were you stranded upon the disabled ship before being rescued?"

"As it so happened, we were only there a mere matter of hours. Apparently Captain Drake had previously arranged for our rescue."

"Captain Drake seems to have had his plan very well laid out."

"You have no idea," he muttered under his breath.

"Nothing has turned out as we had thought it would. Whatever will become of us now?"

"Do not fret, my dear. Things have a way of turning themselves around." He patted my shoulder in an attempt to comfort me.

I sighed heavily. "Will we have enough coin to book passage to return to our home on the island?"

"There will be no need of that." He smiled down at me.

"No? Has the new Duke of Devonshire given permission for us to stay here on his good graces? I do not wish to be considered a charity."

"No, no, my dear. It is nothing of the kind. You see, the Duke of Devonshire wishes to honor his father's marriage contract."

"What?" I asked in disbelief.

"He has asked for my permission to marry you in his father's stead. And I have agreed. We are to leave for his estate in Devon in the morning."

Chapter 35

We were to be married in the chapel on the grounds at the Duke's estate in Devon. The coach rambled along the snow-covered roadway and gazing out of the window at the frozen countryside, my heart seemed just as cold. How could I be a wife to a man I had never met, especially when my heart belonged to Edmund? I looked at my father sitting across from me. He was smiling and seemed so happy. I knew this match was the only way we would survive financially, yet I couldn't help but wonder if I was the only one unhappy about it.

"You look so sad, my dear," he said, placing his hand upon mine. I couldn't bring myself to tell my father of my feelings for Edmund.

"Father, it's just . . . well, things have happened so quickly. The tongues of the gossips will surely be wagging now. Wentworth Simmons is not even cold in the grave, and I am to be married to his son."

"When have you ever given a care to what the gossips have to say?"

"This is certain to bring a dark cloud to my new husband's reputation."

"I sincerely doubt he gives a care to that."

"It's more than that, Father."

"What troubles you, Catherine?"

"I don't know him. The Duke. When I was to be married to the old Duke, I had months to come to terms with it and had the opportunity to become acquainted with him. Now,

I'm to be a wife in a matter of one day. Married to a man I have never met, never seen. Father, I do not even know his name."

"Now, now, Catherine. Calm yourself and lay your fears to rest." He patted my hand.

Silence filled the coach for a few moments, and then I asked nervously, "What is he like, Father?"

"Who, my dear?"

"Why, the Duke, of course."

"He is young, a fine-looking gentleman. Trust me, my dear, you will be pleasantly surprised." He smiled, then under his breath, he muttered, "I know I was."

Then he turned and struck up a conversation with the Contessa in whispered tones.

The coaches drew up to the Duke's estate, a large stately home that seemed to have been connected to an old keep. The tall stone turret and hall were not only intact, but judging from the smoke that curled from the many chimneys, appeared to be in fine working order and still in use.

Our trunks were delivered to our rooms and we were given ample time to relax and to unpack our things before dinner.

My room was decorated in much the same fashion as the room in the London residence. Mary immediately saw to the unpacking of my things. And although I was surrounded by so much activity, I felt isolated and as if I was merely going through motions. I was filled with a sadness I could not overcome. Edmund occupied my every thought. How could I possibly marry someone, a young man I had never met, when my heart belonged to Edmund?

The Duke was notably absent at dinner, which only added to my rattling nerves. I was to be married in the morning to a man who had not even seen fit to present himself for the briefest of introductions before making me his bride and taking me to his bed. The thought of our wedding night brought on another worry in and of itself. Fooling an old man into believing I was still an untouched maiden was one thing, but attempting to fool a young man was entirely another matter. I was certain the young Duke would expect me to be virtuous, as did his father. What on earth was I going to do?

I feared I would not be able to go through with it. I stole a glance toward my father. I knew he counted on me to honor his word and rescue us from financial ruin. Perhaps it was expected that I would be a wife in name only. *What if the young Duke never takes me to his bed, and I find I am with child from my encounter with Edmund at the celebration?* Thoughts swirled around in my mind, and a knot of nerves churned in my stomach. I slid my untouched dinner plate aside.

The conversation around the table grew lively, yet I could not bring myself to participate. I sighed, trying to come to terms with the idea of being forced into yet another loveless marriage. I tried to cast all thoughts of what had happened with Edmund and the possible consequences from my mind.

After dinner, I was not in the mood to sit and exchange pleasantries, so I retired to my room. When I entered my chamber, I was surprised to find a warm fire burning in the hearth and despite the fact that Yuletide was nearly upon us, fresh flowers sat in a vase upon the table. But my eyes were drawn to the beautiful lace-covered white gown that hung on the front of the large dressing cabinet.

The beauty of the dress seemed to lure me to it. Intricate beading was sewn over the bodice, creating a rich and delicate pattern. "Where did this come from?" I said aloud.

"The Duke sent it." I spun around at the sound of Mary's voice. "Ain't it the most lovely gown ye ever laid yer eyes on?"

"I have to say I believe it is."

"I heard tell his mother wore it when she married the old Duke."

"You heard that, did you?"

"Aye."

"From whom?"

"Oh, I don't be recallin' at the moment, but it come with this here box."

She handed me a black velvet box, and I took it with trembling fingers. Opening it, I found a pearl and diamond necklace and matching earrings. The memory of sitting with Edmund on the rocks of the deserted island the day he gave me the oyster and showed me its treasure stung me, and I swallowed the lump that rose to choke me.

"These are lovely," I uttered in a hoarse whisper.

"Miss, sometimes ye just gots to trust in fate. All will be well. You'll see."

That night I could hardly sleep and when I did, my dreams, as always, were of Edmund. In as much as I dreaded dawn, at the same time I sought its relief. I woke in tears, knowing we would never be together. I couldn't help but wonder if he even knew I was now going to be married to the young newly named Duke. I couldn't help but wonder why he didn't step up to prevent it. Why hadn't he come to me after the old Duke had died and ask me to marry him? I couldn't help but wonder if he had lied, stolen my virtue, and most of all, if he ever really cared for me at all. Overcome by such a profound sadness, I could no longer hold back my tears.

Mary helped me bathe and dress that morning, but now standing in my room in the Duke's keep and as she fastened the beautiful pearl necklace around my neck, tears came to her eyes.

"What is it Mary? What's wrong?"

"Oh, it be nothin', Miss. It's just, well, I been takin' care of ye since ye was a babe and well, here we are on yer weddin' day dressin' ye to meet yer husband. I know ye be sad, Miss, but take heart."

"Mary, there is no need to cry. You will be with me many more years. And by the way Tobias looks at you, I'm sure we will be seeing your own wedding day soon enough as well."

"Aye, Miss, I am overly fond of him," she said.

"I know you are Mary, as he is of you."

"Truth be told, just last night, he asked me to be his wife." She blushed, then lowered her eyes.

"That's wonderful news, Mary. I think you make a good match." I hugged her. Tears threatened to spill again when I realized her marriage to Tobias would take her away from me, and she was the closest thing to a mother I had ever had. But I forced them back. "Now, no more tears."

"No more tears. But Miss, the hour be now upon us, and I be certain everyone be in the chapel waitin' on ye."

"Well, we'd best not keep them waiting a moment longer." I smiled and gave her a hug.

The chapel was located in the older portion of the house that remained part of the castle. I stood in the vestibule dressed in the beautiful white gown, fidgeting. A wave of nausea struck me. How could I have allowed this to happen? Standing here about to walk down the aisle and take vows with a man I have never even met was unthinkable. Yet there seemed no way out of it. *I can't go through with this, no matter how much my father is depending on me, no matter how much I love and respect him. No matter how much I wish to honor his wishes, I simply cannot do it.* Lifting my gaze to my father, I whispered, "Father, I'm afraid I cannot go through with this."

"Of course you can, and you will. You have nothing to fear, my dear. You have braved so much, and today you will begin a new life. A good and happy life."

"But, Father, I do not even know this man. All I know of him is the kindness he has shown to me by allowing us to stay in his home in London and the gowns he has gifted me with, despite not ever having met me." I still could not bring myself to tell my father I was in love with Edmund.

"Then you already know him to be a fine and generous gentleman. What more do you need know?"

"Father, you've met with him. Please tell me he is at least not deformed or hideous?"

He chuckled. "I have already told you he is a handsome young gentleman. Trust me, you will be pleasantly surprised."

"Father, can you tell me his name?"

At that moment, the doors to the chapel opened, and it was time to face the stranger I would call my husband.

Walking slowly down the aisle with my hand resting upon my father's arm, the first person who came into view was the clergyman. He was dressed in bishop's robes and looked very pious, despite his wide smile. Then my eyes shifted to the right, and I saw Tobias Smith standing there in his fine dark coat. *Tobias Smith? What was he doing standing there?* My gaze shifted to the man I would marry. My fingers trembled as I took in the figure of the tall man standing next to Mister Smith. The Duke stood with his back to me. His long dark hair gleamed in the light despite being tied back with a black ribbon. His dark coat stretched across broad shoulders, and the cut of the coat accented his narrow waist and slender hips. His dark trousers stretched down to cover long legs and seemed to melt into the tops of shinny black boots. I took in the sight of him, and the memory of the first time I ever saw Edmund swept into my mind and tears stung my eyes. *You love Edmund. You cannot marry this man.*

Panic rose in my throat. Suddenly my feet felt stuck to the floor and I stopped walking. I couldn't move. Father leaned in and whispered, "What is it, Catherine?"

"Father, I cannot. I cannot go through with this. I am in love with another man. My heart belongs to Edmund Drake," I whispered through my tears.

"Trust me, child," he said, and with a stern grip of his hand, he encouraged me to keep walking.

The tall man in the dark coat turned to face me. His gaze wandered over me, and a tiny grin captured just the corner of his lips when his sparkling green eyes met mine.

My heart soared. "Edmund," I whispered. I could not contain the tears of joy rushing down my cheeks, though he had some serious explaining to do.

Despite having a few friends and family members around me, I stood there before the bishop in the beautiful stone chapel with sunlight streaming through the stained-glass windows, looking into the eyes of the man I loved and feeling that we were the only two people in the world.

"Who gives this woman to this man?" the bishop asked.

"I do," my father answered, his words catching in his throat as he spoke.

When Father placed my hand into Edmund's, my fingers tingled at the warmth of his touch.

I'm dreaming. I must be, I thought as I turned to accept my father's kiss upon my cheek. Tears pooled in my father's eyes and his lips quivered.

"I love you, Catherine. Be happy, my girl," he said, his voice cracked with emotion and barely above a whisper.

"I love you too, Father, and I am happy, so very happy."

I turned back to face Edmund, his green eyes dancing with excitement, and the bishop began the ceremony.

Complete joy filled me as I spoke my vows to love and cherish Edmund and he vowed the same to me. The bishop spoke to us about the sanctity of marriage, but his words became a blur as I gazed into the longing eyes of the man who stood before me.

Emotion choked me when he slipped the band of gold upon my finger and I could not find my voice. My fingers trembled when I slid the matching golden ring upon his hand. Unshed tears pooled in my eyes and as I lifted my gaze to meet that of my husband's, I saw his eyes glistened as well. The sound of my fluttering heart rushed in my ears when the bishop pronounced us to be married. Edmund leaned in to kiss me. His soft lips touched upon mine with a promise of a lifetime of love.

After the ceremony, everyone gathered in the great hall of the keep and a feast fit for a king was laid out before us. Musicians played soft strains of delightful music, but when they began to play the melody Edmund and I had first danced to on the ship, I couldn't help but smile. My husband smiled, too.

"Catherine, my love, would you dance with me, here before our family and our friends?" he asked softly.

"I would be honored."

He swept me into his arms, and, holding me close, he slowly swirled me around the floor. Taking my hand in his, he placed it over his heart.

"Catherine," he whispered, pulling me deeper into his embrace. "I think I have always loved you."

"Not always, Your Grace."

He raised one eyebrow at my use of his title.

"From the very moment you tossed that goblet of wine in my face, I knew I loved you. Yet you must realize, my plan was never to fall in love."

"No? Do tell, Captain Drake."

"When word reached me that you were to be married to my father, I developed a plan to abscond with you and force my father to name me his heir apparent and allow me my title. You see, when we became estranged he denounced my claim to the dukedom, so coin had never been the ransom I sought."

"And you think Blackbeard dastardly? I dare say, Captain Drake, your action rivaled his."

The laughter that erupted from Edmund's chest was music to my ears.

"If you loved me from the start, dear husband, then why did you not make your feelings known to me?"

"Without my title, I had little to offer you. You deserved more than a life as the wife of a Privateer. As much as I loved you, I wanted you to have the life you deserved. I convinced myself I could let you go. Then Blackbeard took you from me, and I discovered that he had ordered the Contessa to train you as a courtesan, and that he planned to auction you off to the highest bidder. I prayed he had not compromised you in any way, and I devised a plan ensuring I was not outbid."

"Despite his devious plan, Captain Teach was very kind to me. Although his appearance is quite fearsome, after a while I no longer feared him. My only fear was what my treatment would be once I was sold at the auction."

"I was frantic at the very thought of it. I would have killed him with my bare hands if I had found . . ." His voice trailed off and his jaw tightened.

"Husband, do tell, how did you come to know what the highest bid would be?"

"I didn't. Because I knew my face would be recognized by Blackbeard, I was forced to send Mister Beckett in as the emissary of the Duke. As you may recall, he submitted a sealed bid."

"I was so nervous that night fearing my fate after the outcome that I hardly recall much of the evening's activities. Yet I do seem to have a vague memory of hearing the mention of a sealed bid."

"In it, I promised Blackbeard that should Mister Beckett not prevail in winning the bid, the emissary of the Duke was prepared to pay double the amount of the highest bid of the night in order to win the prize."

"Indeed a ransom."

"And worth every penny, I might add."

I rested my head against his heart, as he swirled me around the room. *I must be dreaming.* I closed my eyes, listening to the strains of the waltz, and the steady beating of my husband's heart. My thoughts were interrupted by the rich laughter of the Contessa, which brought a smile to my lips. For all of her flamboyance and quick temper, she had managed to steal a place in my heart.

"Edmund, how is it the Contessa came to be with my father?"

"After we had taken Blackbeard, we raided his hideout and found her there. She begged asylum, so we took her with us. I knew your father was aboard the ship coming to London. I merely saw to it she was on the same ship and let nature take its course."

I allowed him to swirl me around the room and grew thoughtful.

"What troubles you, Wife?"

I smiled. "*Wife.* I like the sound of that."

"As do I, yet I will not abide my beautiful wife to carry concerns."

"It's nothing."

"Tell me, then."

"I wonder how it is you are known as Edmund Drake, when you are in fact Edmund Simmons?"

"Allow me put your curious mind at ease, wife. My mother was Victoria Drake Simmons. Drake seemed the most logical choice when I became estranged from my father. I harbored such anger for so many years, it pained me to be called Simmons."

"It all makes sense now." I grew silent for a moment and then continued. "I'm thankful you and your father reconciled your differences before his death."

"As am I. Not only did I regain my father and my title, but I gained a beautiful bride as well."

He danced me around the room in silence, holding me tightly. I closed my eyes and relished the feeling of being in his arms. My mind returned to the days I spent at Hartington House, awaiting the arrival of my father and my marriage to the Duke. A smile curled my lips as I recalled the empty cup of cocoa in my room.

"Edmund, was it you who enjoyed my hot cocoa in my chamber at Hartington House every night?"

"Ah, you have found me out, Wife. I couldn't stay away from you. I recalled the nights I watched you sleep when aboard *The Lady Victoria* and allowed myself the same privilege while you were a guest in my home."

"It wasn't a dream then that night I awoke on the ship? You were in the cabin, watching me sleep. Oh, Edmund, you dreadful beast," I teased.

"Even then, I couldn't stay away from you. Catherine, my love, will you ever forgive me for what I have put you through?" He brought my hand to his lips and planted a soft kiss upon my knuckles as the music softened and the dance drew to an end.

"Husband, I shall allow you the remainder of your days to make it up to me."

Even though the music had stopped, he held me close and gazed into my eyes. The conversations and laughter of our family and friends embraced me, and my heart fluttered.

"Now, my beautiful Duchess, now that I have married and am settling down, perhaps we should retire to our chambers to start working on that brood of children you once suggested." His whisper sent a thrill through me, and I smiled up at him.

"It would be my pleasure, Husband, but would you kindly allow me a few moments to ready myself?"

"Certainly, my love. You go on ahead, and I shall join you once I have made our excuses to our guests and bid them all a good night."

When I reached our bedchamber, I was surprised to find the Contessa waiting for me.

"My little'a stick," she said and pulled me into her embrace. "I can hardly believe you a married woman."

"Me, either. Oh, Contessa, I am so happy you are here with me," I said, and I meant it with all my heart.

"I have a little something for you."

She led me to the wardrobe cabinet and removed a sheer white lace garment, similar to the black one she had worn the night I sat hidden behind the curtain in her chamber.

"I also bring you something else, and I hope they survived the trip."

She hurried to the bathing chamber and when she returned, she held an arm full of blood red roses.

"If a man no hungry, he no eat, no matter if that man is a Duke or no."

I giggled and, smiling, gave her a hug.

She tore the petals from the roses, and I lit the candles making the room ready, just as she did that night I helped her at the hideout. After aiding me out of my wedding gown and into the gossamer garment, she placed a kiss upon my cheek and said, "I know you finally happy. Now, use what I teach you to make that husband of yours happy." And she swept from the room in a swirl of skirts and fragrance.

Lying there in the center of the bed, in a pool of blood-red rose petals, butterflies danced in my stomach. But any thoughts of nervousness vanished when the door opened, and Edmund entered the room. He had already shed his dark coat, and making his way to the bed, tossed his shirt among the scattered rose petals along the floor. Standing beside the bed his gaze roamed over me.

"One of us is very much over-dressed, Madam, but I shall remedy that."

I giggled at his comment.

Sitting on the edge of the satin coverlet, he removed his boots and trousers and I marveled at the beauty of his strong and perfect body.

When he took me in his arms and brought his burning kiss to my lips, the heat of deep desire flowed through me.

Although we had made love that night at the ball, savagely, urgently, hungrily, tonight felt like it was our first time . . . our beginning. He seemed much like a nervous lad, and I felt the sting of a blush at the thought.

His tongue ran over my lips and my mouth yielded to him, his tongue exploring its depths, dancing sensually and slowly with mine. His hands slowly drifted to the shoulders of the lace garment I wore, and he tenderly slipped it from me. His lips followed his hands, leaving a trail of warm, wet kisses along my neck. His warm hand cupped my breast as he gently sucked my nipple into the hot depths of his mouth. Already panting with need, I ran my hands through his hair, gently encouraging him to continue.

He raised his head to look at me. "Catherine, this night, let us not hurry. Allow me to worship your body, to give you the pleasure you surely deserve," he whispered as he ran one hand down to caress the dampness between my legs. I whimpered when he stroked me gently. His soft lips moved from my breast and followed the trail of his hand. He planted warm kisses down my body, stopping only a few moments as he licked his way down to my navel. With one hand, he gently rolled a taunt nipple between his fingers, while with the other he rolled the throbbing bud between my legs.

My hands stroked his shoulders and played in his hair, while his head moved lower along my body. I quivered in anticipation.

The hand that had been lavishing attention to my breast now traveled slowly down the length of me, his touch igniting a fire at each caress. He moved lower and nestling between my legs brought his kisses closer to the heat of my core. I felt his warm breath against the soft hair at the vee between my legs. His fingers continued to taunt my bud, and I squirmed with the thought of what he was about to do. He drew his fingers away from my wetness, and I lay there panting.

"You are so beautiful," he whispered, and when the heat of his whisper touched the wetness between my legs, it sent a shiver of delight through me. He allowed his tongue to slowly travel up the inner thigh of my right leg, but stopped short of my throbbing center.

"Edmund," I whispered.

"Yes, my love?"

"Please, you are torturing me."

"Nay, my love, I am pleasuring you. Have patience."

"I wish to give you pleasure."

"You will, my sweet, but your pleasure before mine."

He ran his tongue up the length of my inner thigh and blew a soft breath against my nub, but did not touch me. He placed his soft wet lips everywhere but where I yearned to feel them, where I most wanted to feel them. His warm hand cupped my bum, and he drew me closer. He slid his tongue quickly over my throbbing nub, just barely touching it, and I thought I would explode. His kisses ran again down my thigh. His fingers played in the damp hair between my legs, but he did not touch the folds of my womanhood. Finally, he ran one finger along the wetness and slid it deep into me. A soft moan slipped from me. His tongue ran up along my thigh, and I could feel his hot breath against my womanhood.

I thought I would go mad with need when finally he allowed the tip of his tongue to swirl around my nub all the while sliding his finger into my sheath. I looked down to the source of my pleasure and found him gazing up at me, watching the erotic ecstasy play out across my face.

I cried out in pleasure as he gently sucked and nipped at my throbbing bud. I was thrashing with need, when he continued to run his tongue along my slick folds and gently suck at my nub. His fingers moved faster as did his tongue. I moved my hips in time with him, praying he would never stop. My heart thundered in my ears, and I screamed as my body quivered in release. But when my release came, he covered my wetness with his mouth to drink of my essence.

He slowly slid his body up the length of mine. He rested cradled between my legs yet held himself above me. I felt the length of his hard shaft rubbing against my inner thigh, yet he held himself back and did not allow himself to enter me.

He planted warm wet kisses along my breast and gently sucked one nipple into his mouth. Releasing it, he exhaled softly, the gentle breath causing my nipple to tighten and driving wet heat to the center of my womanhood.

He allowed the tip of his rock hard shaft to rub into the folds of my wetness. But when I lifted my hips to drive him into me, he pulled back.

"Patience, love," he murmured, and he planted more wet kisses along my neck on his way back to my lips.

He ran his tongue over my lips and slowly drew my lower lip into his mouth, then my upper lip as he rubbed the tip of his manhood against my bud. I drew my legs up around his waist, yet he still held himself away from me.

He kissed me then, slowly, his tongue exploring the depths of my mouth. One hand caressed a breast as he rolled his palm over my hard nipple.

Frantic with need, I ran my hands down between our bodies. I felt I had to touch him or I would burst. My fingers wrapped around his hard shaft. Applying gentle pressure, I stroked him. He pressed forward, rubbing my nub with the tip while I stroked him. He groaned. I raised my hips to draw him into me, but again he pulled back. I was drowning in a sea of pleasure.

I placed my finger on the sensitive area beneath his balls and rubbed gently. He groaned again with pleasure. Moving my hand back to his shaft, I placed my fingers around him with slightly more pressure and stroked him. Pulling him toward me, I rubbed the head of his manhood against my bud.

A fierce growl rumbled from his chest and in the next instant he was inside of me. Deep inside. Thrusting in and out of me, hard and fast. I kept my fingers around his shaft, now wet and slick from my essence. He was moving like a wild animal, possessed with a passion I have never thought existed. And I, also possessed by the same wild passion, moved with him.

Together our hearts thundered. Our breath was raspy and quickened. We were climbing a mountain of ecstasy and we both cried out when we reached the apex of our climax, together. I felt as if I had no bones left in my body and I was floating on air laying there beneath him. He kissed me gently, tenderly, raining kisses along my neck, my cheeks, and my eyes. He gathered me into his arms and rolling to his side, he held me close, stroking my back and cradling me to him.

"I love you," he whispered.

"And I love you."

"Catherine, I shall spend the remainder of my days loving you and giving you pleasure," he whispered.

"Is that a promise, Your Grace?"

"Aye."

"Is there a pirate in my bed?" I giggled.

"Funny, I was about to ask you the same question, for only a wild female pirate could love like that," he replied, holding me tenderly in his arms and nuzzling my hair.

"Perhaps I shall have to hold you ransom," I teased.

"You already do," he whispered.

And as I lay there in his arms, basking in the afterglow of our lovemaking, I knew I was the one who had claimed the ransom. The ransom paid willingly and completely by this man who held me so tenderly, the ransom paid to me by my pirate husband . . . his heart.

CPSIA information can be obtained at www.ICGtesting.com
Printed in the USA
BVOW02s1324070813

327619BV00009B/102/P

9 781619 352186